I'M NOT THERE

Jo—
It was great to meet you—
Your designs are outstanding

Jo —
It was great
to meet you —
our designs are
outstanding

I'M NOT THERE

MATT LONG

LIFE RATTLE PRESS

Copyright © 2013 By Matt Long
First published in Canada in 2013
by Life Rattle Press, Toronto, Canada.
All rights reserved. No part of this publication may be
reproduced or transmitted, in any form by any means,
without permission of the author.
ISBN 978-1-927023-49-5
Life Rattle New Publishers Series 1713 8981
Printed and bound through CreateSpace.
Second Edition

Open yourself to new music.
You never know what will catch your soul.

THANK YOU

Lisita Romero

Mark Ferrari

Mom & Dad

Professor Guy Allen

Matthew Del Mei, Andrew Dmytrasz,

Steph Kolodij, & Justin Lau

Errol Gonsalves

J.D., Kerouac, & Buk

Bob Dylan

Patti Smith

I'M NOT THERE

Side One

Chapter 1

Thom raised his rum and Coke over the center of the table in his parent's basement. Carolina and I, seated across from Thom, placed our own identical cups against his.

We clinked the glasses as Thom said, "Here it is: To the greatest summer of our entire lives."

I swallowed, leaned my head on the pink insulation lining the top of the wall, and counted the freckles on Carolina's cheek. Under the table, Carolina's hand crawled into mine. I patted my bare feet on the green, gritty rug under the table. I gulped down another sip of the rum and Coke. The alcohol sent a warm, welcome surge through my body.

Side One

Thom placed his glass with a heavy, striking thud onto the table. He cleared his throat. Curly brown bangs covered his eyes until he swept them away. He grasped his drink and grinned at me.

"Can you believe it's not even May yet? Think about everything we can do this summer. UofT might have been a pain in the ass, but this four month break nearly makes up for it."

"Sure," I said, "Except we're stuck in Paterson. Honestly, I don't know how you could move back home after living on Residence. There's nothing to do here."

Thom laughed. "You two managed to make it, so it can't be so bad."

"Yeah, you're right. It's just... fuckin' Paterson, right? I guess we've got to make the best of it."

Thom chuckled and stood up. He grabbed his glass. A white chip in the dark wood marked the table at the edge of the wet ring left by the glass.

"Anyone else down for background tunes?"

"Nearly twenty minutes," Carolina said, "That

must have been the longest you've ever gone without bringing up music."

Thom walked across the room and entered the TV area, where a congregation of couches faced a mounted 54" widescreen TV. He plopped down in front of the cabinets under the TV and opened two doors. A discordant army of vinyl record sleeves filled the space. Thom pulled a record out and laid the thin square onto his lap.

"Admit it, Thom," I said, as I set my gaze back onto Carolina, "After living in Toronto, it must be a buzz kill moving back to Paterson, right?"

Thom slurped his drink. He wiped beads of Coke from the curly hairs of his light beard. He slid the record back into the line-up and flipped through a few more.

"As boring as Paterson can be, Paterson's home," Thom said. "And either way, I'll be busy this summer, so the suburbs won't bring me down."

"With what?" Carolina asked, "Did you find a job?"

Thom smirked before he shook his head and

Side One

said, "I'm recording an album. I'll choose about ten songs I wrote during the school year and I'll write some more in the mean time. I've got the songs and the time so for better or worse, it's happening."

Carolina smiled and said, "That's awesome."

I nodded. "It's about time, brother."

I scooted my chair towards Carolina, wrapped around her shoulder, and gently rubbed her arm. I leaned my head against hers. Her hair smelt like her pomegranate shampoo. I stared at the chip in the table.

Thom strutted back, sat down, and gulped the rest of his drink. He placed the empty cup beside a paper towel held down by the stir spoon, which fluttered from the breeze of the air conditioning.

A familiar warm tune swam from the speakers before a single drum beat blasted and the Beach Boys "Wouldn't it be nice?" surfed from the surround sound speakers.

Thom wiped his mouth and said, "When will we ever have four months off again? We've got to take advantage. We should all do something special with our summer."

Thom clapped his hands. His voice slurred softly as he said, "Each of us say something we want to make sure happens this summer. Carolina, you start."

Carolina drained her drink. The empty glass thumped onto the tabletop.

She shook her head and said, "I really hadn't thought about it. I just want to relax and hang out when I'm off work. Keep it simple. I'm just happy to be here."

I laughed. Carolina glanced over with hurt printed in her eyes. I finished my glass, leaned to my side, and ruffled open the plastic grocery bag on the cold cement floor. I pulled out a 26er of Bacardi white rum by the neck. I slid the bottle to Carolina. She twisted the silver top off, poured a shot into her cup, and handed the bottle back to me. I poured myself a shot.

I turned to Thom.

"Coke?"

A grin grew on his face.

"I won't go until you answer the question."

Side One

I shrugged. "I don't know, honestly. I guess I want to hike at some point."

Thom laughed, stood up, and crossed the room. He passed his cluster of instruments and opened a door on the back wall of the basement. Thom's hand fumbled on the inside wall until he found the light switch, flicked it on, and entered.

I stared at the chip in the table as Carolina wrapped her palm on my knee. She rubbed it softly until she ran her arm up my leg, over my stomach, and onto the hairs at the back of my neck. She kissed my cheek, my shoulder, and my chest. I kept my eyes locked on the chip, wondering if Thom made it today or sometime in the past, and wondering what to do with my summer, and–

"What's up with you today?"

I turned to Carolina, shrugged, and shook my head. "I'm alright. Probably just still recovering from my exam."

Thom shut the door behind him, sauntered across the room, and set four cans onto the table.

"Alright," Thom said, "It's my turn. Besides re-

I'm Not There

cording the album, I want to ... I want to learn a new instrument. Either the banjo or keyboards."

Carolina rolled her eyes.

"It's your turn again, Carolina."

Carolina crossed her arms and said, "I really don't know what I want."

She turned to me. A small smile spread.

"Actually, I do know. I want to see Trevor's smile every day this summer. Every single day."

Thom turned to me. "You better watch yourself, brother. The line is thin between girlfriend and obsessive maniac. Who know's what she'll do to see that smile."

I snorted, shook my head, and said, "I think I can handle her."

I snatched a can of Coke and cracked it open

Carolina poked my rib cage. I winced. She smiled and said, "It's your turn, baby boy. What do you want?"

I dumped the Coke into the cup. The black, bubbling liquid engulfed the clear rum.

I reached for the stir spoon but Thom already had it clanking against the sides of his own drink.

Side One

"I do want to write more," I said, "Every day, if possible. I've got to get back into the habit."

Thom nodded. "Like at the beginning of each class in Grade 12 Writer's Craft?"

I nodded.

"Righteous," Thom said. "Alright. Anything else you want to do with your summer's, boys and girls?"

"Oh!" Carolina yelped. "Actually, there is one thing I really want to do this summer. I'm on a waitlist for the Biddhuani Retreat, which I hope to hear back from in the next couple weeks. My name is pretty far down the list so the summer session is unlikely. It sucks because it's the only session that, time-wise, makes sense for me."

I shrugged. "Hopefully you can go. If not, that's good too."

Carolina pulled back. A strand of hair fell over her eye as she glared at me.

"Good? Why would it be good?"

I smiled. "The selfish part of me would miss you too much."

Carolina crossed her arms and looked down.

I'm Not There

"Sure."

Thom put down the spoon. I snatched it and plunked it into my cup.

"What the hell is this Retreat?"

Carolina turned to Thom and said, "It's a meditation retreat. All you do all day is meditate. Perfect relaxation, if you ask me. If I do it right, maybe I'll become enlightened."

I placed the spoon onto the napkin, slid the foaming glass over to Carolina, and cracked open another Coke. Carolina handed her glass to me and mouthed a thanks.

Thom drummed his hands against his jeans. He leaned his head back for a second before he pointed to Carolina and said, "Well, I hope you get the chance to go. A meditation retreat. That really sounds wicked. You could be a shaman or something soon enough."

Carolina smirked. "And you'll be a rock star with your album."

"How about you, Trevor?" Thom said. "What are you going to be by the end of summer?"

I looked down at my folded hands in my lap. I

Side One

shook my head and frowned.

"I really don't know what to do. I- I actually thought about making an album, maybe, but I-"

Thom's eyes spread wide and he said, "Let's get you a rock and roll album! We'll be rock stars together!"

"What was the but for?" Carolina asked.

"Don't you think it might be overkill for both of us to record albums at the same time?"

Carolina shook her head. "Just do what you want to do, baby boy."

"Exactly," Thom said, "Listen to the woman. Let's both record albums this summer."

"Unless there's something else you want to do more," Carolina said, "It's your summer."

Thom slapped the table and said, "Come on, something other than rock and roll for our brother, Trevor? Use your head, Carolina."

"Screw you, Thom," Carolina snapped back.

Thom laughed.

I cracked open a Coke and filled my cup to the rim. "I just don't want to let the summer go to waste. I don't want to be in the same place four

I'm Not There

months from now, having done nothing to show for it."

I grabbed the spoon from the ragged, spotted napkin and plunked it into my drink.

"I suggest music if you aren't sure what to do," Thom said, "Music is in our souls."

"It isn't so easy for all of us," I muttered.

Thom shrugged. "Let me know if you want to make an album. You and I could do something real trippy, I bet."

I shook my glass in my hands, watched the bubbles evaporate, and looked back up at Thom.

"You know what Thom, let's do it. Let's make an album. Making music could be exactly what I need this summer."

I slipped a notebook from my pocket, flipped the worn down brown cover open, and found a fresh page near the back. I pulled a pen from the pocket at the front of my plaid dress shirt. I set the pen onto the page and scribbled, "Plan and duty for summer- Record the most rock and roll album since *Dig Lazarus Dig*."

Side One

I shut the notebook and shoved it into my tight pocket.

Carolina smiled. Her hand crawled into mine. With her other hand, Carolina raised her rum and Coke over the center of the table. Thom and I placed our filled cups against Carolina's.

Carolina said, "To summer," and we clinked our cups.

Chapter 2

My head leaned on my fist as I scrolled through an Internet biography of James Joyce. The blinds behind my office desk shut out the bright morning light. I checked the clock at the corner of my computer screen.

11:50.

Ten more minutes.

Tickets for the 3rd annual Urban Picnic Festival went on sale at noon. Every summer needed a good music festival, and the Urban Picnic remained one of the few in Toronto. The ten minutes separating me from those tickets felt like an eternity. I wanted to order an extremely limited

Side One

VIP package that, last year, sold out within five minutes. The package included a signed T-shirt, two CDs, access to a VIP section with two drink tickets, bleacher seating, and an opportunity to win backstage passes.

11:51. Nine more minutes.

I stood up from my desk chair and crossed my office. The room belonged to Jack, my brother, until he moved into the basement a few years back. I knelt down in front of a black bookcase beside the door, ran my fingers across the plastic jewel CD cases on the bottom shelf, and grabbed Animal Collective's *Strawberry Jam*. I stood up and crossed the room, back to my desk.

The CD player sat on the top shelf of a black vertical-running cabinet wedged between the desk and a waist-high brown speaker box. I pressed the power button and the disc port slid open. I dropped the CD onto the black tray, pressed play, and the CD drive swallowed the disc.

An old man whispered "Bonefish." Synthesizers seized and a heartbeat throb pumped from

I'm Not There

the speakers. I turned up the volume.

I flicked on a lamp at the top right corner of my desk. I grabbed a pen and scrawled "Summer Plans" in the center of a blank page in my notebook. I circled the words and drew a line sticking out from it. As I scribbled "W" at the end of the line, the doorbell chimed through the house.

I stood up and lifted a window shutter. The bright rays of the sun beat into my sore eyes as I scanned the empty driveway. I dropped the shutter, paused the stereo, and checked that the button on my crotch was fashioned. I left the room and walked downstairs.

A blurred round figure stood on the other side of the glazed window in my front door. I swung the door open. The blur transformed into Carolina.

"Hey there," Carolina said, through a smirk.

She stepped in and pecked my unwashed lips.

"Morning babe. Nice to see you this early."

Carolina knelt down to untie the laces of her purple sneakers. After she tugged her second shoe off, I held her hand and pulled her up. We

Side One

crossed the main floor to the kitchen.

Carolina planted herself on a chair at the granite island. I opened the fridge.

"You want anything to drink? The options are... Milk, water and a few beers."

"Beer, please. Or water."

I shut the fridge and opened a cabinet. I grabbed a Batman cup and pushed it under the lever on the "freezer" half of the fridge. Clumps of ice cubes clinked as they tumbled into the cup. I pressed the "water" button and pushed against the lever until the cup filled.

I passed the glass to Carolina, sat beside her, and said, "Why are you out this early?"

"I had nothing to do so I figured I'd see what you were up to."

"Fair enough."

I wrapped my hand around Carolina's soft cotton sweater. My eyes flicked to the clock on the oven. Four minutes.

"Is it alright that I'm here? You aren't working on your album, are you?"

I sipped from her glass.

I'm Not There

"No, I was just watching TV."

Carolina placed her hand on my leg. I turned to face her. She inched towards me. I half-smiled before our lips connected. My eyes shut as my hand clutched onto her sweater. My heart thumped against Carolina's chest and my hand crawled underneath the bottom of her shirt.

Carolina pulled apart and whispered, "Wait."

We left the kitchen, crossed the hallway, and ascended to the second floor.

I opened my bedroom door and moved aside to let Carolina in. She passed me and spread herself on top of the brown comforter. Carolina's hand lay behind her sea of brown hair. I shut the door and all light disappeared.

I crawled onto the bed, over to Carolina, and found her lips. I stroked my hands through all that great soft twisted hair and her hands grappled onto my back and my leg wrapped around hers. I pulled our lips apart and panted as I tore off my glasses and placed them between an empty mug and a radio alarm clock that glowed "11:59".

Side One

I swung over and placed my hand on Carolina's rosy cheek.

"I'll be right back."

Carolina's smile dropped.

"Where are you going?"

"I've just got to go to the other room for a minute. I want you to be exactly there when I get back."

Carolina sat up, crossed her legs, and frowned.

"There's only one thing you could possibly need to get at this moment," she said, "And I know those are in the drawer right there."

I shook my head and said, "It's not that."

I turned to the clock. 12:01.

"What does the time matter?"

"It doesn't."

Carolina got off the bed and stood in front of me with her arms crossed.

"Trevor, what are you up to? I won't let you leave until you tell me. Or bring me with you."

She stared me down, trying to withhold from blinking.

"Alright, let's go."

I'm Not There

I turned around and twisted the knob on the door. The bedroom flooded with light from the hallway. I entered my office and sat down at the desk chair. Carolina pulled a stool up beside me.

I refreshed the Internet screen and the Festival's home page loaded anew. I clicked on "Order Tickets" — a newly revealed feature — on the top right corner of the page.

"Really?" Carolina cried out, "When?"

"June 20th. Just a bit over a month from now."

"I'm kind of disappointed it's earlier this year but whatever. What day is the 20th?"

"Should be a Saturday."

"Oh fucking right," Carolina said. "Now, when the hell were you going to tell me about the show?"

"When I saw you tonight."

I ordered two VIP package tickets.

"Why the hell didn't you tell me before?"

"I wanted it to be a surprise," I said, "But that didn't go according to plan."

"It's still really nice, Trevor. Who's playing?"

"No one that exciting, to be honest."

"That's alright. It's more about the experience."

"Exactly."

"But still, who's playing?"

An apology page loaded. "The requested tickets are not currently available."

Shit.

I returned to the previous page and ordered two general admission tickets.

Within a minute, the tickets were confirmed.

"Alright, you and I are officially going to the Urban Picnic Festival."

Carolina squealed, wrapped her arms around my shoulders, and kissed my neck.

Carolina whispered, "Thank you," before her head turned back to the screen.

"What now?" I asked.

"You've got anything else you need to do?"

I smiled and kissed her.

Chapter 3

I pulled the black CD binder from the back seat and handed it to Carolina.

The light turned green. I stepped on the gas pedal. The maple leaf air freshener danced under my rear view mirror.

Carolina opened the binder, skimmed the familiar page, and flipped to the next page. The binder held 64 MP3-file CDs. Each disc contained anywhere from two box sets to twelve albums.

Carolina folded her hands over the CDs. "Honestly, I don't know. Suggest something."

I shrugged. "It's a gorgeous day. How about the Velvet Underground?"

Carolina rolled her eyes. "Always the Velvets."

Side One

I snickered. "If you don't like it, you pick."

She huffed and flipped a few pages ahead.

I pressed the stereo's power button. The black screen flashed and green lines formed the word "Welcome". The screen sat blank as it waited for its CD injection.

I returned my eyes to the road. Two cars drove side-by-side fifteen feet ahead.

"Still no rap, huh?"

With a smirk, I said, "No, everything but."

"I still don't get why you have more country than rap."

I shrugged. "Hank Williams and Johnny Cash are both pretty rock and roll."

I rolled down the window. The tropical atmosphere inside my Civic swam out and a cool breeze gushed in. Carolina raised her hand to her flush chest.

"I didn't realize how much I needed you to do that."

I stopped at an empty intersection for a red light. A skunky scent wafted in. I scrunched my nose and rolled up my window. Carolina twisted

I'm Not There

the knob for the air-conditioning. The fans sputtered on and shot warm air from the vents.

I glanced at the binder on Carolina's lap, snatched the CD from the top right corner, and slid it into the stereo.

Carolina shut the binder and asked, "What's this?"

"Keep looking. This is just until you decide. It's a collection of tracks I made from Bob Dylan's *Basement Tapes*. Most of the songs are still officially unreleased but I compiled my favourite's from the sessions. There's a take of one song that is literally his only performance of it. It's practically holy."

A hazy organ seeped through the car. Soon after, Dylan's warm but ragged voice swam in.

"Come on, Trevor," Carolina said, "Not now. It's such a nice day."

I laughed. "What do you mean by that?"

"Oh, nothing."

"Come on," I said, "What does the quality of the day have to do with Dylan?"

"Nothing," Carolina said, "Dylan's great. It's

Side One

just sometimes his voice gets on my nerves. But in small doses, Dylan's great."

I gripped the steering wheel. I turned left through an intersection and kept my signal on. Our destination, Paterson's movie theatre, sat on the other side of the road.

"Are you okay?" Carolina asked.

I snickered. "Yeah, of course. You only somewhat insulted me."

She frowned. "How did I insult you?"

"You don't like Dylan because of his terrible voice and his lazy musicianship, right?"

Carolina shrugged and said, "I hadn't thought about it so much."

"Well," I said, "I don't know how you're going to ever listen to my album because those are the exact qualities I'm bringing to it."

A black truck passed. I crossed the road. The car bumped as it drove into the near-empty movie theatre parking lot.

Carolina pulled one of my hands from the steering wheel and said, "You and Dylan are not the same."

I'm Not There

"You're right," I said. "He's the best writer of the rock and roll era."

I parked in a spot near the entrance of the theatre.

The song ended and the humming guitars of the next song begun.

"Here it is," I said, "That holy song."

Carolina shut the stereo off with a wicked smile across her face.

"Let's go, the movie's about to start."

I checked the time on my phone, frowned, and unbuckled my seatbelt.

Chapter 4

Thom and I strolled into Merrie Melodies, the local record shop. The soft strumming of Joni Mitchell emitted from the speakers above the door. A shield of posters plastered on the front window blocked the daylight from entering. A single light bulb hung at the center of the store, which dimly lit the small room.

Mr. Felling, the store owner, glanced up from his newspaper. His wispy gray hair blew in the breeze of his fan.

"Morning boys," he grumbled.

"Hello," Thom said.

We passed the vast CD sea that swamped the room. Between the "Z" of rock and "A" of blues, a

Side One

set of knobless doors hung shut. A sign over the doorframe read "The Vault."

I pushed against the center of each door. They swung back. Jack White's molten guitar blasted out Joni Mitchell. Thom clapped me on the back as he entered the first aisle of vinyl records: Rock A-M and other genres. I swayed into the opposite aisle: Rock N-Z and new releases.

"You looking for a specific album?" Thom asked. He examined the back cover of a leafy Beach Boys record.

"Nah," I said, "I'm looking for inspiration. I want something really loud and distorted. But I want my album to mean something. I don't want to just create another burden on the world like half these motherfuckers."

"Word," Thom said, "Distortion and noise and all that is great, but acoustic is working for me now. I'm getting a shit load done."

"Oh yeah?"

I shifted to the P's.

"It's rad working with the band, don't get me wrong," Thom said, "But if I could stay home all

I'm Not There

day and write songs, I'd be in heaven."

"You should install a sandbox into the basement. It worked for Brian Wilson, right? I'm sure the 'rents won't mind. At least you use a lot less drugs."

"I should at least ask, right?"

I stretched and yawned. Thom held a Joy Division album open. He squeezed another record under his armpit.

I moved to "S". After flipping through a few records, I uncovered a hellish gem- The Stooges *Fun House*. The cover displayed band members in a cycle of fire. I placed the record under my arm and sauntered to the V's to check for rare Velvets. As usual, the store had none.

"Alright, I'm good to go."

"You find something?" Thom asked.

I raised the record.

Thom nodded and said, "Cool."

We sauntered up the aisles. At the top, Thom handed his two records over.

"Oh shit," I said, "These are sweet."

"Any inspiration there?"

Side One

I shook my head. "I'm not sure we can make anything quite like *Yoshimi* in your basement. I want to cover a song from whatever album I choose."

"True that. But at least *Yoshimi* is on pink vinyl."

I laughed.

Thom nodded and said, "Do you want to go over to my place to listen to them? I've always wanted to hear early Stooges."

"Have you never heard *Fun House*?"

Thom shook his head.

My bulging eyes and huge suction of air exaggerated my genuine surprise.

"We've got to hurry," I said. "Every minute until you've heard *Fun House* is a minute lost."

I pushed the swinging doors and left "The Vault." Felling stood at the "H" section of rock with a stack of CDs under his arm.

He turned to us and said, "You boys ready?"

"Absolutely," Thom replied.

Felling stalked back to the register. He set his stack of CDs onto the counter.

I'm Not There

I placed my record onto the laminated countertop. Felling glanced at the price tag.

"Six bucks."

I pulled out my wallet and a five-dollar bill stuck out.

"Can I borrow a dollar?" I asked. "I don't want to use debit for a buck."

"Better yet, let's just throw them all on the same bill."

Thom set his records on top of mine.

Felling glanced at the stack and said, "Twenty bucks."

"Shit, you serious?" Thom said through a grin.

Thom snatched a twenty from his leather wallet and handed it to Felling. I gave Thom the five-dollar bill.

"Alright boys, enjoy," Felling said.

"Yeah, we'll see you again soon," I said.

"I'm sure."

"So you're cool to come back to my place?" Thom asked. "We can jam if you want."

"If the inspiration comes, brother."

Chapter 5

"See?" I said. "This is what my album should sound like."

Thom nodded along as the Stooges pounded primal noise from the speakers hanging in the top corners of Thom's basement. His feet hung over the sides of the couch in front of the TV. I sat up, my head in my hands, and listened.

The record rotated on the turntable in the red mahogany cabinet under the TV. Iggy howled, the saxophone screamed, and guitars roared until the music suddenly stopped. The speakers hissed in relief.

"Goddamn," Thom said, "This album is a beast."

Side One

Thom clapped his hands and stood up.

"I don't know about you but I'm ready to lay down some rock and roll."

I stood up, opened the cabinet under the TV, and flipped the record over. I placed the needle on the edge. Seconds later, Iggy howled, and the ride through the *Fun House* restarted.

"Really?" Thom said. "Don't you want to jam? We've already heard the album, what, 3 times? How inspired do you need to get?"

"I'm not ready," I said, as I slunk onto the couch, "I can't figure it out, but something's missing."

"Why don't you try another instrument? You could play drums."

"It's not that. I just don't have the songs yet."

"Let's just jam," Thom said. "We're bound to come up with something."

I shook my head. "No man, that isn't how it works. We've got to have real songs first, like the Stooges."

Thom laughed. "Are you serious? The message you get from *Fun House* is to plan every second?

Isn't that, like, the opposite of their message?"

"Shit, you don't know what you're talking about. I've got the complete sessions of this album on a CD box set, and it's amazing how similar all the takes are. They knew what they wanted to do the moment they walked into the studio."

Thom scoffed and said, "You bought the record, even though you've got the complete sessions?"

"Sure. The record and the box set are completely different beasts. The record is the perfect slice of the pie. The complete recordings are everything in the damn kitchen, pots and ingredients and all. But the box set proves those fuckers were prepared, and that's the most rock and roll thing about The Stooges, if you ask me."

Thom laughed. "Okay, here's what we'll do. We'll choose a song and record different layers of it. We'll record our guitar parts first. We can put drums or vocals or whatever we want overtop after. We'll just build the song."

"How can a song be constructed like that? Music isn't Lego."

Side One

Thom chuckled. "Trust me, man, that's just how it's done. Even the Beatles recorded their songs that way by the end."

I shook my head and said, "No, not my album."

Thom reached over, grabbed his guitar, and placed it on his lap.

"Why don't I show you some riffs? I could definitely give you something. I've got enough songs to fill two albums, if I wanted."

"Thanks, but I'm alright," I said. "You know what, today isn't the day. I've got to think about it some more. Let's try again next week."

Chapter 6

Lenny Kaye's electric guitar surged through me as I lay on my office's soft carpet. A thunderous wall of organs rocked behind Patti Smith yelling "Horses, horses". My ceiling fan spun and washed cool air over me. I shut my eyes.

The stereo's sound waves faded away and my entire album unfolded in my mind. Suddenly, a fact hit me: the album needed an organ. With an organ, I could do anything overtop and it would rock. The songs ran through my mind. One melody in particular struck me. I needed to capture it, somehow.

I sat up and spied my acoustic guitar— a lazy excuse for a music-making machine— leaning

Side One

on my desk. With an organ, I bet I'd already have a rock opera released.

I held out my hand and strained my back to reach my guitar but it sat a foot out of reach. I relaxed my arm, leaned back, and sat straight.

After a year of lessons, my fingers fell back to the same frets every time I played- the D chord. I needed something else. I needed an organ.

The needle lifted off the record. I uncrossed my legs and heaved myself up. I stalked over to the record player. I picked up the vinyl by the edges and slid it carefully into its cardboard shell. I flicked off the speakers.

The melody I needed to capture played from a gramophone record player at the summit of my mind's mountains. The needle skipped over the rotating disc and approached the edge.

I twisted my body and searched for something to capture the music with. I relented, stood up, and wrapped my hand around the neck of the acoustic guitar. The silver strings scratched my fingers. I dragged the computer chair to the center of the room and sat down. I faced a gray

I'm Not There

poster of the Beatles.

I strummed the D chord. My song sat somewhere in the vibrations. I sensed it. I strummed again. The out of tune strings made even the D chord sound wrong. I pulled the guitar off my knee and leaned it against the cabinet.

I shut my eyelids and listened for the melody.

I have to read "Ulysses" one day.

The song evaporated into the cluttered airwaves of my mind.

I opened my eyes and dug my foot into the gray carpet as I stood up. I picked up the guitar and leaned it against the wall behind the big brown chair in the corner of my room. When I sat down at my desk, the chair blocked the guitar from my eyes and my mind.

Chapter 7

The car sped past the strip plaza with the local pub, Izzy's. My sunglasses glazed the world over with a green-gray coating. I gripped the warm leather of the steering wheel. A stream of icy air conditioning shot out of four open vents on the dashboard.

We stopped at a red light. A cop car sat at the other side of the intersection. The seatbelt held back my chest as I stretched my stomach with a gulp of air. I shut off the air conditioning. We sat in silence until Carolina flipped the CD binder to the last page. The binder sat on her outstretched leg. Her foot pressed against the glove compartment. She twisted a CD so my green scribbles

Side One

faced the correct direction.

"Where do you even find these bands? Without you, I swear, I never would have heard of any of these artists. How can I know what CD to pick if I have no idea what anyone sounds like?"

"Name me something."

"Hmm... The Hold Steady. Who are they?"

"I haven't made you listen to them yet? Shit. Well, to be honest, they're really rock and roll, so you might need a few listens before you can digest it."

Carolina flipped the page.

"Okay. On this CD, you have Nick Cave, The Smiths, Lou Reed, Neutral Milk Hotel, and Tom Waits. How about any of those?"

"Goddamn," I said, "That must be the most depressing line-up I could've made. They're all way too dark for a beautiful June day like this."

"See, Trevor. My first six picks, you don't suggest. You should just choose for us."

I checked the rear view mirror. No one approached from behind. I switched to the turning lane and flicked on my signals. The stoplight at the approaching intersection glowed red.

"We made an agreement," I said. "You pick the CD and I pick the restaurant."

I turned onto Iroquoi Blvd, a long curving connection between the newer suburbs and old Paterson. The car sped around the bend.

"Why don't you pick the CD that sounds most like your album?" Carolina said

"Actually, I had the idea the other day that my album needed a lot of organ. I know you don't want Dylan, but he does use organ on almost every song."

Carolina flipped a page back and said, "What about The Doors?"

I cleared my throat and said, "Actually, The Doors would be perfect."

Carolina smiled and wrapped her arm around mine.

"Do you have any of their CDs in the car?"

"I don't know. Check. You should be able to decipher the writing if you know what you're looking for."

Carolina flipped the binder to the beginning.

Side One

She sat silently while she read the artist titles on two pages of disc.

I stopped for a red light. Condos with whitewashed bricks and closed garage doors and deep green lawns stood on the other side of the street.

Carolina flipped to the third page and asked, "What are we going to do after dinner? Can we go back to your place?"

The red light switched to green. The car accelerated. We passed the condos. Treetops brought shadows over the sidewalks. An apartment building with dirty brown bricks towered into sight. Foreign flags hung off every third balcony.

"My parents have friends over. I actually told Thom we would go over to his house at some point."

"Oh. What are we going to do? Work on your album?"

I shrugged and raised a half-smile.

"I don't know babe, we didn't discuss it. We'll probably work on the album for a bit, but not all night. We'll watch a movie or something."

Carolina flipped through the binder.

I'm Not There

I reached the next intersection, turned right, and immediately switched into the left lane. I crossed the empty street into a shopping plaza.

Carolina pulled a CD out of the case.

"Save it for the drive to Thom's house," I said, "We're here."

Chapter 8

Carolina leaned against the red bricks of Thom's house. She fanned herself with one hand. The other hand held the straps of her purse, which sat on the concrete porch.

I rang the doorbell again, dropped my hand to my side, and slipped my car keys into my pocket.

"Did you book this Saturday off for the Urban Picnic?"

Carolina shook her head and said, "I'll do it as soon as I go in tomorrow."

"Okay."

Carolina nodded and said, "I will."

"I believe you."

I looked down. "I really don't want to work on

Side One

the album today. I'm just not feeling it."

"So don't," Carolina said. "Do what you want."

A knock pounded. I jumped. Thom peered through the glass window in his front door. A goofy smile stretched across his face. Silk curtains fell back over the window, the door unlocked, and it swung open. Thom's eyes reflected his fire-fighter shirt.

"Welcome," Thom said and stepped back.

Carolina stepped into the house. I followed. A glittering chandelier hung over our heads from the ceiling of the second floor. Carolina placed her purse onto a short wooden bench and kneeled to untie her sneakers. I slipped off my shoes.

"What's up brother?" I asked.

Thom shut the door. My sweaty skin crystallized in the frosty atmosphere.

"Just working on a new song and I feel pretty good about it. I think it could be the opener for my album. Would you two want to hear it?"

Carolina stood up and said, "Yeah, sure."

"You down to go out for a walk first?" I asked.

I'm Not There

Thom shook his head.

"I'm good. I went half an hour ago."

We followed Thom down the rotating staircase and through the open door at the bottom.

Carolina and I lay on a green couch he recently retrieved from a garage sale. It sat against the wall closest to Thom's corner of the basement. Scattered around his corner, which occupied the entirety of a large blue rug on the concrete floor, were two acoustic guitars, three electric guitars, a drum kit, a banjo, an electric piano, a tiny amp for his old blue Fender, and a newer, wider amp.

Thom sat on a faded brown kitchen chair in front of the couch. He tuned his guitar, strummed, and twisted the pegs more. Thom strummed again, straightened out his back, and pushed his curly bangs from his face.

"I just wrote this in the morning so I'm still working out the kinks."

Thom cleared his throat. He rearranged his hand around the guitar neck onto new frets and strummed. After a pause, the song picked up with a bouncy beat. Thom's ethereal voice soared

Side One

in.

Four minutes later, wooing and tapping his leg, Thom struck hard on the guitar, ran his hand down the neck, and pressed down to stop the ringing strings.

Carolina clapped.

"Bravo sir!"

I nodded rapidly.

"Yeah man, that was really good."

"Thanks," Thom said, "It's not quite done but I like it. It's going to be like Pavement meets the rhythm of the Talking Heads. The recording will probably have doo-wop harmonies over top."

I laughed and said, "Fair enough."

Thom leaned his guitar against the foot of the couch.

"Why don't you two play something with me?"

"The only thing I play is violin," Carolina said, "And I doubt even you have one hiding around."

"Violin?" I said, "You play the violin?"

"I started playing when I was nine. I only stopped when I moved here from the States."

I'm Not There

"So it's been... five, six years since you've played?" Thom asked.

"Yeah, something like that."

"Well shit, still," Thom said, "That's impressive."

Carolina shrugged.

"How about you Trevor?" Thom asked. "You down to play?"

I sat up and rested my feet on the scratchy rug.

"I'd rather not. I still don't have anything. I might have to learn a new chord if I try."

Thom shifted in his seat. He scanned the ensemble of instruments.

"You could try the drums. It might be fun to just beat 'em."

My foot tapped against the rug. I looked down.

"You know what," I said, "I'm alright where I am."

I sunk into the couch and wrapped my arm around Carolina.

"Play us something else," Carolina insisted.

Side One

Thom saddled the guitar onto his knee.

"What do you want to hear?"

Carolina shrugged.

"Doesn't matter."

Thom strummed. His smile dropped.

"I don't understand what's going on with this damn guitar. It falls out of tune between every song."

I patted my shorts slowly.

"Oh shit," I said, "Have you figured out if you can make it to the Picnic on Saturday?"

Thom's wide eyes bore into mine.

"You won't believe it. I checked the website yesterday. The festival sold out. Who the fuck would have thought?"

"Wow," I said, "It'll be huge compared to last year then."

"I guess so."

"Can you play "Rocky Raccoon" again?" Carolina asked.

Thom chuckled. "Again? How many times have you heard me play that?"

"Must be a million but it gets me every time."

I'm Not There

Thom strummed the guitar.

"Alright," he whispered, "Here goes."

"And then we'll go for a walk after?" I said.

Thom laughed. Carolina's hand grabbed mine.

Thom struck the opening chord and rambled out the song. Carolina sat up straight and stared at Thom. She snorted at his vocal inflections. She whistled along with the "doo do doo" section in the middle. Her legs tapped with the beat. When the song concluded, Carolina clapped and cheered for an encore.

Thom put down the guitar with a grin across his face and stood up.

"Let's go?"

Carolina and I followed Thom upstairs.

Chapter 9

Carolina and I lay atop mesh chairs beside the still pool in my backyard. A cluster of brown birds perched along my fence bantered in harsh, quick squeaks. Flowers lined the bottom of the fence. An empty patch of soil where tomatoes failed to grow sat at the end of the row of flowers.

I reached over to the checkerboard patio table, picked up my beer bottle, and sipped a cool swig.

"Will you swim if I go in?" Carolina asked.

"Of course."

Carolina got up and stretched. Her black T-shirt rose, revealing her pale stomach.

"Okay, I'll get changed then."

Side One

Carolina crossed the porch and entered the house.

I sipped more beer and stretched my other arm behind my head. I raised the bottle to my lips for another sip when beeps carried over from the table. I stretched my neck and spotted Carolina's vibrating phone.

I hesitated. I gripped my bottle, bit my lip, and got up. I checked the caller ID.

Unknown number.

I grabbed the phone and slid the glass door open.

"Carolina!"

Her voice muffled by the bathroom fan, she said, "Yeah?"

"Your phone's ringing," I shouted.

"Bring it to me... Please."

I passed through the living room and knocked on the powder room door. Yellow light glowed through the crack underneath.

Carolina unlocked the door. The knob turned and the door cracked open. I passed the phone through. She thanked me and shut the door. I

I'm Not There

heard muffled conversation before I returned to the backyard.

I waited, topless, for a few minutes. When the door slid open, Carolina wore the same clothes as when she entered the house.

"You'll never guess who that was."

"Your secret boyfriend?"

"Very funny," Carolina said, "No, that was the Biddhuani Retreat!"

"Oh, what did they want? I thought the session already passed."

Carolina sat on her lawn chair. I swung my body to face her.

"They just opened a new session because of the demand. They asked if I want to attend."

"Amazing," I said. "When is it?""

Carolina lowered her head.

"It starts this weekend."

"Seriously? That's outrageous. Who calls that soon before?"

Carolina's leg churned into the porch.

"I know, right? Well…"

"Well, what did you tell them?"

Side One

"I told them to reserve a spot for me. I want to go, Trevor."

I nodded slowly. My head fell a bit further with each bob.

"What about the Festival?"

"That's what kills me, honestly. I really don't want to miss the concert with you."

I shifted and said, "There's the matter of the ticket and the money…"

"All that can be figured out. I want to go with you. I've been dreaming of going with you. But I'm scared I'll miss out on something important if I don't go to the Biddhuani Retreat."

"Is this the only time that you can go?"

"Kind of. This session makes the most sense. If I don't go now, it's either Christmas or next year. I don't want either of those."

A bullhorn blasted. The cluster of birds burst off the fence. Their wings fluttered with a violent fury as they disappeared to congregate in another yard.

"I want you to do what you want to do."

"I know," Carolina said, "But will you be okay

I'm Not There

if I don't go with you?"

I sighed and looked down at the cement porch. Grass emerged from a crack in the cement.

"Sure," I said, "No problem. I'll ask Thom if he wants your ticket."

"He said he wanted to go, after all. I'm sure he'll be able to."

"Yeah, I'm sure he will."

"Are you really sure you're okay if I go? I totally understand if you're upset. I just want you to be honest."

I masked myself with a smile and nodded.

"If you want to go, go for it."

Carolina leaned over and threw her arms around me. She whispered, "Thank you. You are the best."

She pulled back and stood up.

"I'm calling Simon now. He won't be impressed that I need the week off, but screw him."

Carolina walked to the side of the house.

I set my beer to my lips but I didn't feel like drinking. I put the bottle down and hoped the birds would return.

Chapter 10

The same note shot over and over from the speaker beside my big brown plush chair. I got up, stretched, and staggered across the office. My back ached from my awkward sleeping position. I leaned over the metallic record player.

The last groove of the record locked the needle in. The sight of the vinyl — usually a spinster for freedom but now stuck in perpetual motion— freaked me out. I lifted the needle and placed it on its latch. The spinning stopped. I grabbed the vinyl and slipped it back into its sleeve. I wiped my eyes and sat down to pick a new soundtrack.

When I passed Neil Young's *After the Gold Rush*, I knew I found it. I slid the record out,

Side One

placed it on the record player, and brought the needle to the edge. The needle locked in and the acoustic guitar leaked out.

It felt like Neil sat right there, playing his guitar just for me. But he wasn't. These chords rang forty years ago and that Neil grayed out.

I leaned on the carpet. I tried to avoid the thought that raced over and over through my mind until it overwhelmed me.

Trevor, you're wasting time.

I got up and sat at my desk. I flicked the switch on my lamp and the bulb burst on. My house and car keys clung to the left edge of the desk, about to plunge into a fifteen-minute, panic-stricken quest. I snatched them and tossed them onto the cabinet beside the record player. The keys landed on the edge of a black dinner plate with a turquoise candle at the center. I turned back to the desk and tapped on the edge along with the music.

You're wasting time, Trevor.

I picked up my pen and wrote without thinking. I wrote about not having anything to do,

I'm Not There

which was the truth. My free time contained as much as a balloon with a hole poked into the side. After blathering for a page and a half, I wrote my real question in the center of the page.

"What am I supposed to do?"

I wanted to write all the other questions that rooted from this one, but I couldn't. In even larger letters, I scrawled,

"What am I supposed to do?"

I got up and passed the big brown chair. I picked up the acoustic guitar that leaned against the wall. I sat on the brown chair and placed the guitar on my knee.

I decided not to turn off Neil. Either way, I couldn't play well. His presence could only help.

I formed the D-chord and strummed. Still out of tune. I slid my hand down and made up a chord. I strummed. It sounded all right.

Every time I saw Thom, he had a new song to show. Every single time.

I put the guitar down. If music was Thom's path, good for him.

I sat at my desk and picked up my pen.

Side One

I wrote again in big scrawling letters,
"WHAT THE FUCK AM
I SUPPOSED TO DO?"
I put the pen down and closed my notebook.
Fuck it. I'll figure it out tomorrow.

I slid open the big drawer on the left of the desk. Notebooks filled the drawer. Some notebooks were thick and bulbous. Others only had forty short pages. Loose sheets of paper stuck out of a bunch. The metal spindles of most pointed upwards. The book in my hand already had its spot at the end of these notebooks. Another notebook would come after. I didn't know what it would look like. I didn't know what words would mark its pages. But that notebook would be there soon enough, and another after.

I closed the drawer. I opened my notebook to a fresh page. I picked up my pen and started writing a story that lingered in my mind all week.

It was a memory of Carolina and I at the Paterson harbour. Amongst a crowd of people, a homeless man leaned against a tree. Carolina didn't have anything less than a ten so she gave

I'm Not There

him that.

I finished the first paragraph and stopped.

I turned around, ready to chuck my pen, but I spun the chair back and tightened my grip. I exhaled slowly and put my pen to the page.

An hour later, the story filled seven pages. The blizzard of words amazed me. I got up, flipped the record, and dropped the needle. I sat at my desk, turned the story back to the first page, and opened my laptop to type it up.

Chapter 11

Two Years Before

As far as I could see, an endless blur of plaid lined up to enter Fort York for the first annual Urban Picnic Festival. Most men had beards, scruffy buttoned up dress tops, and fluorescent shorts that didn't reach their knees. The women dressed the same.

A light breeze carried conga drum beats over from the stage a few hundred feet away. I gazed at the guardrails set up to guide the crowd towards the stage.

If she isn't here in two minutes, I'll go back to the stage. If I wait much longer, I'll be stuck near

Side One

the back, behind the speakers. I've got to meet Thom soon. Carolina probably couldn't make it. She probably couldn't get a ticket. She only said she'd try. I'll just wait until I see her tomorrow and ask her then. That will be better anyways.

I raised my hand to my forehead to block the sun. I scanned the line again. I took in a deep breath, held it for a few seconds, and released it. My left hand raced nervously over my stomach.

A finger poked into my ribs. I turned and Carolina stood before me. She wore a blue and white striped shirt. She tied her straight hair into a ponytail.

"Hey!" I said, "How did you get by me like that?"

Carolina smiled. "A woman has her ways."

I laughed. "Appareantly so. I can't believe it worked out."

I stuffed my hands into my pockets as we followed the crowd towards the stage.

"Did you get in alright?"

"You'll never believe it," Carolina exclaimed. "I got in for free!"

I'm Not There

"Seriously?" I said, "How the hell did you do that?"

"I'll tell you later. But as I said, a woman has her ways."

"Shit, no doubt about that."

We reached the back of the crowd. Carolina pulled me right into the middle.

It took the sets of two bands, during which a heavy rained crashed for ten minutes, but we finally stood only a few feet from the front of the crowd. Four bald, bulky black-shirted security guards patrolled the space between the guardrails and the stage.

Carolina stood in front of me. Her shirt clung to her body. Her hair, once straight, now curled freely over her shoulders. I leaned over to her and said, "Do you know the next two bands, before City and Colour?"

"No, who are they?"

"Cat Power and Animal Collective."

"Oh, awesome," Carolina said. "What do they sound like?"

Side One

"Cat Power is a female solo singer. Pretty indie. She'll be good. Animal Collective are hard to describe but I've seen them before and they're great."

Carolina turned back and smiled. "Then I can't wait."

Carolina's hand found mine and our fingers melded into each other's.

A roadie tested the main microphone. Two minutes later, he exited off stage. I leaned to Carolina's ear but I pulled back. I felt trapped by the horde of people. I almost suggested to leave until Carolina leaned back and said, "Is that Monica and Thom up ahead?"

She pointed off to the right.

I stood on the tip of my toes and looked towards where she pointed.

"No," I said, "That guys hair is way too short to be Thom."

"Where do you think they are?"

"I don't know. I can text him."

"No, I was just wondering."

I'm Not There

Carolina smiled. "Thanks for inviting me today, Trevor. This was the best first concert ever."

The crowd erupted into applause. A thin woman in a green top and short brown hair walked to the microphone. A band of men dispersed over the stage and picked up instruments.

My heart thumped hard. I bit my lip. I inhaled a deep breath, held it, and released. I leaned next to Carolina's ear.

"Carolina, can I ask you something?"

Carolina's head turned. Before her lips parted, I said, "Do you want to try dating?"

Without pause, she said, "Of course."

I put my hand on her cheek. She leaned in and kissed me with her soft, sweet lips. After ten seconds, we pulled apart and I opened my eyes.

Carolina turned around as Cat Power began her set. I wrapped my arms around her stomach, squeezed, and never let go.

Side Two

Chapter 12

"Welcome back," I whispered.

"It's so nice to see you, Trevor, you have no idea."

We pulled apart and Carolina's warm, small hand fell into mine.

"Tell me all about the retreat. How was it? What was it?"

Carolina shut the door. "Take off your shoes first. The night's early."

I wriggled off my black sneakers and grabbed ahold of Carolina's waist. We swerved around her pink suitcase and black duffel bag, which lay at the foot of the staircase to the second floor, as we left the entrance. We passed through the

Side Two

family room, where a lonely green couch and a pristine tabletop meditated, and we entered the living room. Wires dangled from the TV mounted on the wall over an electric fireplace. DVDs and mugs sat on a crowded glass coffee table. I slid my backpack off and leaned it against the couch as Carolina shut the blinds.

Carolina and I sat across from each other on the couch, our legs wrapped around each other's waists.

"Tell me all about the retreat."

Carolina looked down. Shortly after, she said, "Sorry, I'm just tired. I explained the trip to my parents and my sister separately already."

Carolina inhaled deeply and exhaled slowly.

"It was simple, in a way. I meditated for nine to ten hours everyday. We had to stay silent the whole time. We weren't even supposed to look at other people, especially the boys. All we were supposed to do was meditate."

"Ten hours? Shit…"

"It wasn't ten hours straight. We took a break every few hours. But still, ya know? They held an optional morning meditation at 6:00, but I slept through that, obviously. By the end I only ate a slice of toast and maybe some apple for breakfast. But, as you know, I'm allergic to apples so I could only have a slice or two. I prayed for pasta but it didn't come until the eighth day. I don't know why but I figured pasta was something they had."

"And that was the trip?"

"Basically. Breakfast, meditate, break, meditate, lunch, meditate, break, meditate, dinner, meditate, and the day is done. I feel great though, really. Absolutely refreshed."

"I don't know how you pulled it off."

Carolina sighed. "I won't lie. I had a really hard time at first. Really hard. I wanted to quit and I nearly did. But by the fourth day, I got used to it. The trip was far from easy, but I had to finish."

"Goddamn," I said, "Well I'm really proud of you. That sounds intense. I would have quit, no doubt."

"Thanks," Carolina said, "But tell me, how was your week? You made it, I see?"

Side Two

I squeezed her hand.

"Barely, my lady, barely."

"What did you do? Work on your album at all?"

"Oh no," I said.

I leaned, grabbed my backpack, and unzipped the main pocket. I pulled out a black duo tang and handed it to Carolina.

Carolina's eyes squinted before she flipped the cover back.

"Reaching for Ten? What is this?"

"It's a story I wrote. The first of many, I hope. While you were gone, I made the decision to write a book instead of recording an album."

"Really? You won't finish the album?"

"What's to finish? At this point, I'd rather just write a book."

As Carolina stared at the story, her lips spread into a small smile.

"Do you have any idea what the book will be about?"

"Vampire romance. I need a best-seller."

"You haven't got a clue, have you?"

I'm Not There

"Well, not much about the content. But I want it to be a minimum of 200 pages. The title will be one long word and it will fade across the cover."

"That's what you've decided so far? You know I love you but your one idea is a bad idea."

"I just know I probably won't have time to write and finish a novel, if I'm being honest with myself. But I could settle for a short story collection. It would have to be at least fifteen stories though to make 200 pages, right?"

Carolina shrugged and said, "Do you have any story ideas?"

"Oh sure, a few."

Most centered on Carolina but I felt like I couldn't tell her. I wanted her to just have the stories, without any build up.

"It's going to take a lot of time to get it done," I said, "Between brainstorming, writing, and editing."

"I can't wait to see what you create."

Carolina flipped through the pages. At the end, she closed the folder, threw her hands around my neck, and lay her head on my chest.

Side Two

The story dropped to the floor.

"I missed you, poop," Carolina said.

"I missed you too, baby blue."

Carolina shut her eyes.

"So what do you want to do tonight?" I asked.

"This."

"Oh," I said, and snickered, "Fair enough."

I moved my hand under her shirt and grazed bare skin.

"Did you want to go out later on, though? It's been a long time since you've gone out and done anything."

"Yeah, but it's been as long since I've done this. Can we please just relax tonight?"

I put my head down and sighed.

"Yeah, sure."

Carolina raised her head.

"Trevor, what was the sigh for?"

"Nothing."

Carolina stared into my eyes for a few seconds before she rested her head on my chest.

"Let's just have a good night. I haven't seen you in a long time."

I'm Not There

"Alright," I said.

Chapter 13

I pulled a green aluminum bottle from the main pocket of my backpack and passed it to Carolina. She unscrewed the lid and held it over her mouth.

The sun snuck in and lit patches of the crunchy pebble trail. I kneeled to relieve my sore, tight legs. I ran my fingers over the pebbles. Light brown dirt stained the tip of my fingers.

As Carolina swallowed another sip, I said, "This is a hell of a nice way to take a break from writing."

Carolina wiped her mouth and offered me the bottle. I shook my head. She screwed the lid back on top and walked behind me. A clink emitted as

Side Two

the bottle struck something inside my backpack.

She zipped it up and said, "Let's go."

We carried on down the dirt path. Up ahead, a man approached. One hand held onto a young boy. The other tugged on the tight red leash of a Rottweiler. The dogs snout surveyed the ground.

Carolina's hand latched into mine. She pulled us to the edge of the path. Brittle leaves of short trees ran across the back of our necks.

A few feet away, the Rottweiler's head shot up and its beady black eyes moved back and forth between Carolina and I. The dog snorted, snarled its black lips, and roughly pulled at the leash. The boy tripped with the force. Deep barks escaped rapidly.

A whimper escaped Carolina. Her nails dug into my arm.

The man tugged on the leash. The dog yelped but continued its relentless barks.

I shielded Carolina and hurried in the opposite direction. When we passed the dog, I pulled her in front of me and held onto her stomach. I heard the dog get smacked and it released a cry.t.

I'm Not There

Carolina still clung to my arm minutes later.

"Are you alright, babe?" I finally asked.

Carolina shook her head.

A snicker escaped. "No?"

Carolina pulled her hand off my arm.

"No."

"I still can't believe you get so scared of dogs."

"Did you see that thing? That dog would happily rip our faces off and eat our toes for a snack."

"If it was only big-ass dogs like that, I'd understand it."

Carolina looked forward while her head bobbed.

"But when it's some poodle yapping at you and your heart skip a beat, that's when–"

"Trevor, stop."

We walked quietly for a few moments. The trees blocked the sun from breaking through, yet it somehow remained bright.

"I understand strays, but doesn't a leash make it better?"

"Hell no. Dogs must hate being tied down and feeling controlled."

Side Two

"This is Canada, Carolina. The dogs are domesticated."

Carolina stopped. I stood in front of her. She crossed her arms and frumped her face.

"You're a jerk, Trevor. I had a bad experience with a dog as a kid. Not all dogs are the lovable friends you Canadians know them as."

"Do tell."

"No."

I sighed.

"Fine. Dogs can be scary. I just don't get it. I had a dog, remember?"

"Yeah, I remember that dog, Trevor. His bark scared the hell out of me."

"Yeah but he's a bad example."

Carolina looked around. She nodded to the path's edge, where the trees stood thin and the tops of trees peaked from the bottom of the valley.

"Let's get off the path," Carolina said.

"And go where?

"Let's climb to the bottom of the valley. Why not?"

I'm Not There

"Why not?" I said. "Really? Why not? Because that hill is steep as hell."

Carolina shook her head, grabbed my hand, and dragged me with her.

"There isn't anything on this path except dogs and assholes. Let's go down the valley and be rid of both. Okay?"

I laughed.

"Alright," I said, "Lead the way, you asshole."

Carolina punched my arm and said, "No, I want you to take me down."

I leaned over and looked down the hill. The trees spread sparsely.

"You ready?" I asked.

"Yeah, let's go!"

I sighed as I grasped her hand. Our other hands held onto coarse tree bark as we started down the hill.

Twigs cracked and leaves crushed underneath our slow descent. The shorter, younger trees blocked our upward view until only a blanket of leaves covered our heads. My feet felt unsteady but I held onto the tree trunks tightly.

Side Two

The splashes of a creek a few feet away sputtered when we reached the bottom of the hill.

Carolina looked around and walked in a small circle with her head tilted up, her hair falling in a woosh towards the soil.

"This place is heavenly," she whispered.

My neck craned further back as I followed the ascending tree trunks.

"How old do you think these trees are?" I asked.

"From the looks of them… I'd say 636 years, 11 months and 12 days."

I turned to her; my eyes squinted in puzzlement.

Carolina's laugh escaped. I accompanied it with my own.

A few feet away, a bush shook. Carolina and I followed the noise.

A small garter snake shot out of the bush and slithered for a few seconds before it disappeared into another bush.

I grappled onto Carolina's arm and raised myself onto the tips of my toes.

"Fuck this," I said.

Carolina laughed. "What's the matter babe?"

"I fucking hate snakes, you know that."

I clutched harder onto Carolina's arm.

"Oh baby, you'll be okay. That snake won't do anything. I won't let it."

"Let's just get away from here."

Carolina and I turned around and hurried away from the spot.

"Trevor, you know that it's literally impossible for that snake to hurt you, right?"

I shook my head, clutched her harder, and picked up the pace.

"That's not the point, Carolina. Snakes are fucking evil. They just slither along without legs, doing whatever the hell they want, eating whatever their hingeless mouths desire. There's no reason with a snake."

Carolina tripped over a branch in the path. I caught her before she crashed completely. She looked up and groaned.

"Sorry," I said, "Are you alright?"

Carolina patted her face and tucked a strand

Side Two

of hair behind her ear. "Yeah, I'm fine. Are you fucking fine now?

I nodded. "I just really hate snakes."

"Yeah but shit, you've got to control yourself."

"Yeah," I said, "Yeah, yeah. You're right."

I grabbed Carolina's hand and pulled her up. We strolled along the valley until we reached the creek. It blocked us from a grassy field, and for as far to the left and right as we could see, there appeared to be no way to cross the river without getting soaked. We watched the river run for a few minutes before we headed back.

"I don't want to stay in here much longer," Carolina said, "The bugs are starting to get to me."

"Alright."

"What do you want to do later?"

"To be honest, I want to go in earlier than not today. I've got to work on my book. I'm already far behind if I want to finish by September with an ounce of my sanity."

Carolina looked down. The grip of her hand loosened.

I'm Not There

"It won't be every day," I said, "But everyone agrees that the two most important things for young writers is to write a lot and to read a lot."

"I'm happy that you're writing," Carolina said, "But it's shitty that it leaves me with nothing to do."

She sighed. "But it's okay."

I looked down the path and wanted to say something but nothing seemed right so I stayed silent.

So did Carolina until we approached the bush the snake retreated into.

"Hopefully there isn't a snake's nest nearby."

My eyes widened.

"Shit, you're right. Let's get the hell back up to the path."

Chapter 14

"Did you like it?" Thom asked, as the final note of his song rang between his basement walls. He locked his guitar between his knees.

I leaned my stool forward and nodded over and over. My eyes remained on a stain in the rug under Thom's feet.

"Solid, brother," I said, "Definitely pretty awesome. What'd you say it's called?"

Thom stroked his beard and said, "Color me shameless. I wrote it last night. I went for a walk, smoked a J, came back and just did it. It must've only taken twenty-five minutes to write."

"Hmm."

Thom got up. "Want another drink?"

Side Two

"I'm good."

"Alright, I'll be back in a sec."

"Alright."

I drank a sip of Coke. I lifted the edge of the red rug with my foot. My foot crawled against the cold cement.

Thom brought a beer back. He twisted the cap off and flicked it behind the floral couch against the wall. He sat on his rickety chair.

"You want to play anything?" Thom asked.

"Nah."

"Come on, brother, you've got to at least try."

"Not anymore," I said, "I'm writing a book instead of making the album."

"Really? What about?"

"Most likely it will be a short story collection."

Thom chugged his beer. He pulled the bottle away and wiped foam from his beard. He patted his leg with his free hand and nodded.

"I feel good about it," I said. "I wrote a few stories so far."

"That's cool. How do you know you're a good enough writer for a book though?"

I'm Not There

I eyed Thom. He pulled the bottle to his lips again. When he swallowed, he said, "I'm just saying. If no one's read them, how do you know?"

"Yeah. Yeah, you're right. I guess I don't know. I always did good in English."

"Yeah, but that doesn't really mean anything."

I lifted the Coke to my lips. My eye got caught in the blaze of the light bulb. My foot tapped against the carpet.

I swallowed and said, "I don't know man."

"Go for it," Thom said, "As you said, you've got to do something with the summer. But if you ever want to finish the album, let me know."

I raised my head and said, "Alright."

"Say, do you want to hear 'Rainbow Rain' again? I figured out a new chorus for it."

I stared into Thom's dark eyes before I lowered my head to hide my frown.

"Sure, why the hell not?"

Thom placed his guitar on his lap.

"I hope you like it."

Chapter 15

"Do you have any Daft Punk?"

I took my eyes off the road and onto Carolina's lap, where the CD binder sat shut. I ran through a mental checklist.

"No."

Carolina opened the binder. She ran her index finger along her silver necklace. A ruby sat in the center of the necklace. I gave the necklace to Carolina as a gift for our two year anniversary, which passed a few days before.

"I don't know what I want to hear," Carolina said.

I spun the wheel and turned onto a two-lane, bumpy side road bordered by high stalks of corn.

Side Two

A sign flashed by. It read "Speed Limit 80 km." I pressed my foot on the pedal.

Our destination, Mount Nemo, stretched out against the clear sky. The Mount Nemo Conservation Area contained one of Ontario's best trails. Trees ran rampant over the winding, bumpy mountain but the outline of the car path along the edge stood out.

"Maybe the Lips?" Carolina asked.

"The Lips or the Flaming Lips?"

"Flaming."

"Yeah, of course. The CD should be closer to the back, if I recall."

Carolina flipped through until the back page lay open. Her finger ran over scribbled names.

"I feel like I'm getting the hang of this book. I still can't find anything I want to listen to, but at least I can read the options."

"That's a step," I said. "Give it time. You'll love it all in the end."

Carolina pulled a disc from the sleeve and slid it in. She tossed the binder onto the back seat. The CD loaded and a guitar screeched. The feedback halted before another rhythm boogied in. The drums loaded.

Embryonic began.

Carolina lifted the lever beside her chair. Her seat fell flat. She shut her eyes and slapped her knees along with the drums.

"That's the difference between us," I whispered along with the chorus.

At the end of the road, I spun the wheel a hard left to follow the winding path up the mountain. The road narrowed to a one-way. I pressed harder on the gas pedal for extra kick but the car lurched along.

The song ended. Carolina lifted her seat. I squeezed her hand. She looked outside. Her hair fluttered in the breeze of the air conditioning.

"This book's just waiting for me to type it up," I said. "I can feel it."

Carolina smiled. She skipped to the next song.

"Sometimes it feels like the only thing I can do is write. That seems to be normal. I forget who it was — I think Bradbury — but whoever it was, he said that by the third day without writ-

Side Two

ing, he felt totally crazy. I think I'm starting to feel the same way."

Carolina stared at the passing trees.

"Sometimes when I'm not writing, it feels like I'm lost."

The road straightened out and flattened when we reached the top. The thick bustles of trees fell back and the road carried on, bordered by a rickety fence, without an end in sight. Plowed lands laid open for cottages on one side and the Conservation area on the other.

Carolina sighed. "Just go home and write, if that's what you want or need or whatever."

I turned my head.

"What? I didn't mean that at all."

Carolina pressed the eject button. The CD slid out. The screen flashed a broken line. She dropped the CD into the cubby under the stereo.

"I only meant to say I feel really good about writing the book. I feel like I'm getting something out of my summer."

The sign for the Conservation Area appeared on the left, tucked behind a wall of leaves. I swerved and crossed the road. Carolina gripped onto the door handle.

When the car straightened, Carolina reached back for the black binder. She placed it on her lap and flipped it open. After a few pages, she pulled out a CD and slid it in. Shortly after, the guitars of the National's "Fake Empire" bore from the speakers.

"It'll be great to get out here and stretch our legs," I said, as I tapped along to the music. "Breathe some fresh air. See some real sights. Maybe I'll get a poem out of it, like Kerouac woulda?"

I patted my left pocket. Wallet.

I patted my right pocket. Lighter. Cell phone.

"Goddammit."

Carolina turned to me. "What's the matter?"

"I didn't bring my notebook."

I exhaled a deep breath and shook my head.

"Its fine," I said, "Just annoying."

Carolina rested her head on the window.

I drove up to the wooden cabin at the center of the road. A young woman with pigtails atop

Side Two

her head slid open the window. I rolled down my car window.

"Hello, hello!" the cashier exclaimed.

"Afternoon."

"Just the two of you today?"

I scanned the empty back seat and turned back to her.

"Yeah."

"Okay. $13 please."

I pulled out my wallet, grabbed a $20, and handed it to the cashier. I thanked her as she handed the change back to me.

"The lot is just up ahead to the left. Park anywhere you like."

I rolled up my window and drove past the erected white gate. It dropped immediately behind us.

Four cars sat in the parking lot. I parked close to the path. I stepped out of the car and locked the doors. A light breeze splashed onto my face.

I sucked in a heavy gulp of the crisp air. I held it in my bulging mouth and turned around. Carolina stared at me, her eyebrows cocked.

I'm Not There

I laughed. The wind puffed out. I walked around the car, kicking pebbles along the way.

I grabbed Carolina's hand and we stepped onto the dirt path, which cut through an open field of grass. To our left, four people stood in a circle far off. To our right, a man pushed a kid on a swing at a playground. A woman sat on a bench at the edge of the playground with headphones in.

"When can I read some of your book?" Carolina asked.

I took my hand and thrust it into my pocket.

"Soon," I said. "Soon. I want to get a decent amount done first. And I can't show you my first drafts. They're shit, pretty much."

"I don't care," Carolina said. "I just want to hear your stories. I love your writing."

"Okay, but I've got to make sure they're right first. I know you don't care, but I don't wanna show you shit."

"Okay baby boy."

I smiled. "You'll be the first reader, baby blue. Or maybe the only one."

Side Two

"Why would that be?"

"They might not be worth anything," I said, "And I don't want to waste anyone's precious time. Except yours, of course."

I walked a few steps before I noticed Carolina had stopped. I turned around. Carolina stood with her arms crossed.

"Come here," she said.

I pointed my thumb over my shoulder.

"But the trails this way."

She shook her head. "Just come with me. Trust me."

Carolina stepped off the path. She stopped underneath a tree's shadow and sat down. I followed her.

"Sit down," Carolina said, "And cross your legs."

I sat down cross-legged.

"We're going to meditate," Carolina said. "You need it."

"I can't meditate."

"I said the same thing before Biddhuani. Trust me, you can do it."

I'm Not There

"I don't know, Carolina, we could just start up the path. I think-"

"Trevor, please just try."

I sighed. "Alright."

Carolina smiled. "So what you're going to do is concentrate on your breath. Sit there and put all your mind's energy on listening to your breath. Feel the air crawl through you."

"What position do I put my arms?"

"Whatever's comfortable."

I crossed my arms. I uncrossed them. I laid my arm on my thighs. Then over each other. I kept switching their position until Carolina said, "You can close your eyes completely or keep your lids semi-shut. And remember to concentrate on your breathing."

"Big or little breaths?"

"Just breathe naturally."

I shut my eyes. Bright spots glittered over the black space.

"Oh, one last thing," Carolina said.

I opened my eyes.

"Straighten out your back, you gargoyle."

Side Two

I straightened my back.

"Like this?"

"Raise your head. They told me to imagine that the tip of your skull is trying to reach the sky."

I sighed, said "Alright," and raised my head to the sky. I shut my eyes.

The grass tickled my legs. I shivered. Wait. I need to concentrate on my breathing. Okay. The air rose through my nose. My lungs lifted. I opened an eye.

"Should I breathe through my mouth or my nose?"

Carolina's eyes stayed shut. "It really doesn't matter. Do what's natural."

I closed my eyes. Okay, I can do this. I stopped thinking. The breaths entered, my lungs lifted, and I exhaled. I inhaled, held it, and exhaled. Inhale. Exhale. Inhale. Exhale. Inhale. Exhale.

Fucking right, Trevor, you got this shit. Inhale. Exhale. Easy as hell. Inhale. Exhale. Inhale. Exhale.

I read somewhere that Ginsberg hummed

I'm Not There

"Omm" when he meditated. Should I ask Carolina if I should? Maybe that's a different type of meditation. Or just a Ginsberg touch. I bet him and Kerouac hiked up mountains all the time. Sat down. Meditated. Went home and wrote the greatest works of the century. No big deal.

Shit. Inhale. Exhale. Inhale. Exhale. Inhale. Exhale.

I raised an eyelid.

Carolina sat with both eyes open.

"What the hell?" I said.

Carolina shook her head before she pushed herself off the ground.

"Let's just walk."

"No, come on, gimme another chance."

She held her hand out and helped me up.

I followed her until dirt scraped under our shoes and I slipped my hand into hers.

We strolled the serene path. The only noise came from the patter of our steps and and the rustling of leaves.

I inhaled the fresh air and held it for a few seconds. I followed the tree trunks and I won-

Side Two

dered how long they stood for and how deep their roots ran.

A deer crossed the path. Its thin brown legs shot it across quickly. Carolina reached for her phone to take a picture but the deer disappeared before Carolina's hand escaped her purse.

A bit further up, a small sitting area opened up. I pulled Carolina's hand and we walked to it. A stone wall along the edge reached my chest. Carolina's chin tipped above it.

On the other side of the wall, a forest valley spewed for miles under the clear sky. The treetops stuck out like arrows in the quiver of the Earth. I squeezed Carolina's hand.

"Beautiful, isn't it? I wonder how many poems have already been written about this very spot."

Carolina coughed. She pulled her hand from mine and raised it to her throat. She coughed again before it cleared. When the coughing stopped, Carolina patted her neck.

"What the fuck?"

My head turned. "What's up?"

I'm Not There

"My necklace is gone."

Carolina lifted her T-shirt and reached between her breasts.

"You're sure you had it in the park?"

"Absolutely."

"No chance it's in the car?"

"Shit, I don't know," Carolina said. "I just know I had it when I left the house."

"Alright. We'll find it. There's no reason to panic."

Carolina turned around and hurried down the path. I caught up with her. We walked in silence. Carolina surveyed one side. I scanned the other.

We walked the entire path without any sight of the silver. When we reached the field beside the parking lot, Carolina sighed. She crossed the grass towards our shady tree. I followed her with my eyes scanning the ground.

Carolina kneeled around her meditation spot. Her hands glided over the grass. I stood over her with my hands on my hips.

Finally, Carolina raised her head. Her eyes were red.

Side Two

"It isn't here. It's gone."

"Do you want to check up the path one more time?"

"We would have seen it."

Carolina stood up.

"Let's check the car," I said. "I'm sure it will be there."

Carolina nodded.

I grabbed Carolina's hand but she pulled it away and stuck it into her jean pockets.

We paced back to the car. I unlocked Carolina's door and she swung it open. She bent down, ran her hands along the seat's sides, and checked under. When the necklace didn't turn up, she sighed and sat on the seat.

"It isn't here."

I licked my lips and shook my head.

"I'm sorry. Why don't we go? This doesn't seem to be working."

A tear streaked Carolina's face. I stuck my thumb out to wipe it off but the tear splashed to the ground before I could.

"Are you sure?" Carolina said.

I'm Not There

"It's up to you."

Carolina's eyes squinted as she shook her head. "Let's go."

I nodded.

Carolina stuck her feet in and slammed the door.

I walked around the car, slipped into the seat, shut the door, and buckled my belt.

"Sorry about the necklace," Carolina whispered.

"Don't worry about it," I said. "Not one bit."

She leaned her head against the window.

I stuck the keys into the ignition and started the car. I ejected the National, grabbed the Flaming Lips CD from under the stereo, and slid it in. The guitar screeched.

I backed up, confirmed no other cars approached, and spun the wheel to bring the car towards the exit. As we passed the wooden cabin at the front, the cashier waved. I nodded to her with a smile and raised a peace sign. I placed my hand back on the wheel.

"What do you want to do now?" Carolina

Side Two

asked. "I hope you don't want to go home."

"We could see a movie."

"Is Thom free? We could go to his house."

"I don't know. I haven't talked to him this week."

"Hmm."

"Why don't you check to see what's playing?"

Carolina pulled out her phone.

Chapter 16

My head sunk into Carolina's plush pillow. I stretched and twisted my legs over the aqua comforter on her bed.

Carolina applied mascara while she looked into a mirror on her feeble white desk. Around the mirror sat piles of Cosmo magazines, nail polish bottles, papers and pens and post-it notes, and her hulking laptop.

The shelves above the desk organized all of Carolina's possessions into sections: a section for her movies, her books, and her make-up ensemble. Posters for Goodfellas, Parks and Recreation, and Peter Jackson's King Kong surrounded a world map over her double bed. A

Side Two

string with dangling plastic planets hung over her headboard.

"I'm going to Moe's to play poker tonight."

A strange look crossed Carolina's half made-up face when she turned to me. Her eyes squinted and her lips pursed. The light over the mirror flickered.

"Really? Since when?"

"He texted me last night. I asked if he'd be down to chill on the weekend, but this is the weekend of their annual Montreal trip, appareantly."

Carolina turned back to the mirror. Her eyes widened as she pushed the small mascara brush through her eyelashes.

"Are you okay if I go?"

"Of course. I'm just surprised you're ditching me for something other than your book."

Carolina stood up and opened the bleached double closet doors behind her. The metal rack held more empty hangers than clothes.

"What are you going to do tonight?" I asked.

Carolina pulled out a black-and-white striped

shirt and held it against her chest. She frowned and hung it back up.

"Why?"

"Well, I like to know what you're up to."

Carolina sighed.

"I don't know, Trevor. I figured we would chill tonight but I guess not."

"Why don't you give Monica a shout?"

Carolina closed the closet door, crossed back to her desk, and sat with her back to me.

"Don't worry about it."

I sat up and hung my legs off the bed.

Carolina turned her head over her shoulder.

"Why did you even come over if you have to leave in an hour?"

"I only need to go in two hours. And it doesn't matter how much time I have. Whatever time I get with you is worth it."

"I don't know. I think you should just go. I've got stuff to do."

"What the hell are you talking about? We were about to hang out."

"Don't talk to me like that, Trevor."

Side Two

Carolina picked up a brush and combed her straight brown hair.

"Sorry. But I don't want to leave yet."

Carolina shook her head.

"Fine. Can you pass me a bobby pin? They should be on the shelf."

I got up and scanned the shelf. No bobby pins.

"You sure?"

"They're there somewhere. Please look."

I shuffled through a stack of papers on the nightstand between the bed and the desk. No bobby pins. I picked up as many pages as possible. At the bottom sat "Reaching for Ten." I picked it up.

"Oh wow, I forgot all about this."

"What is that?"

"It's the story I wrote while you were at the Retreat. How did you like it? You never told me."

Carolina ran the brush through her hair.

"It was really good."

I flipped through the crisp pages.

"Yeah? What was your favorite part?"

"Oh, I don't know Trevor. I just remember

laughing a lot."

I skipped to the second page.

"Strange, I wouldn't describe it as funny. What was so funny?"

Carolina turned her head. "I don't know Trevor, it just was. Did you ever find a bobby pin? I think there's one in the drawer."

I placed the story on top of the stack of papers on the nightstand and opened a drawer. It was filled with pens and papers and, sure enough, bobby pins. I grabbed one, shut the drawer, and handed it to Carolina. She thanked me and stuck it into her hair. I walked back to the bed and leaned against the edge.

"You didn't read it, did you?"

She sighed and put down her brush.

"Did you read it?"

"I started reading it the night you gave it to me. I thought it was great. But then I fell asleep and somehow never got back to it."

I nodded a few times. "Alright."

"Are you mad? Don't be. I'll read it tonight."

"Sure, sure."

Side Two

Carolina put down her brush and smiled.
"Do you want to watch some TV for now?"
I nodded. We stood up and left the bedroom.

Chapter 17

The carpeting of each step to Moe's basement darkened with a thicker layer of cat hair. You turned a corner and a beer fridge took up most of the gap between the two walls. Pizza boxes, beer cans, and bubble wrap littered the floor. Piles of religious DVDs, which Moe's parents sold on the Internet, sat in stacks on the pool table. The pit reeked of spilt beer, unwashed feet, and cat piss. The stale air remained because the builder placed the window too high for anyone to bother opening it. A palate of stains marked the faded walls.

Moe, Owen, Greg, Hank, Thomas and I sat around a square mahogany table in the corner of the room. We piled the empty pop bottles and

Side Two

paint cans that previously covered the table onto a couch. The cards stuck to the table in a few spots but once your nose got used to the aroma, a few hours wasn't so bad.

Owen slammed his cards down and scratched his shaved head. "This game makes no goddamn sense."

I swallowed a swig of beer and said, "Another shitty hand, eh? Well, me too."

I dropped my cards face down.

Thomas nodded, placed his cards down, and tapped on the table twice.

"Me too," Greg said. He dropped his cards, drained his beer, and wiped his mouth on the scarf around his neck.

"How about you, Hank?" Moe asked.

Hank shook his head. "I'm in."

"Alright, flip the cards."

Moe and Hank put their cards on the table.

"Double queen," Moe said.

Hank shook his head. Moe pulled the chips over to his corner and laughed.

"That's the way you do it, boys."

I'm Not There

I got up. "Anyone else need a new beer?"

Owen and Greg asked for one. I walked to the beer fridge, grabbed three, and sat back at the table. I slid the bottles over to Owen and Greg.

"Alright, who's dealing?" Hank said. He scratched his patchy, blonde beard.

Greg leaned back, stretched his hairy arms, and yawned.

"Let's take a break. We've been playing for what, three fucking hours now?"

Owen swallowed his beer and said, "You just can't handle losing."

"Shut the fuck up, bro," Greg said. "You're doing shittier than I am."

"Come on ladies, keep it civil," Moe said.

"Let's just try to finish, alright?" I said.

Owen shook his head. "Nah, I agree, let's take a break.

Everyone drank in silence for a few minutes until I asked, "Are you all ready for Montreal?"

"Hell yeah!" Moe shouted.

"Why aren't you coming, Trevor?" Thomas asked.

Side Two

"Ah shit, I can't afford to go. And I can't just go all of a sudden."

"Shut the fuck up, Trevor," Greg said. "We're staying at my cousin's house and there's still a spot in Owen's car, so gas won't be too bad after it's split. All you'll need is booze and food. Do what you want to do. It's your summer."

Moe stood up. "Gentleman, when we're traveling down Crescent at four AM after drinking from the moment we rise to the moment we drop and we're mowing on poutine every chance we got- well, the only word to describe it is epic. Now, I need each and every one of you to be there for its success. Tell me you're all in."

Moe turned to me with an eyebrow raised.

Owen nodded.

Greg said, "Fucking right I am."

"What's holding you back, man?" Hank said.

I drained my beer bottle. "Alright, what the fuck? I don't have anything I need to do."

"Ahh there we go!" Moe said.

He raised his bottle. "Cheers! To Montreal!"

I clinked my bottle and swallowed.

Chapter 18

I stepped into Carolina's house and shut the door. I shivered. Murmurs rang from the living room.

Carolina called out, "You're done playing so soon, Marco?"

"No, it's me."

I kicked off my shoes and lined them against the false door. I walked down the unpainted hallway, through the family room, and entered the dark living room. Carolina lay on the couch with the remote resting on a green throw pillow on her stomach. Her eyes stayed on the screen.

"Hey babe," I said. "It's nice to see you."

I bent over to plant a kiss onto Carolina's lips.

Side Two

She moved her head aside. I pecked her cheek and walked to the end of the couch. She lifted her legs and I slipped underneath them.

"How was your weekend?" I asked.

"It was fine."

"Did you do anything fun?"

Carolina shook her head and squeezed the green throw pillow to her chest.

Homer tried to build a barbeque. Instead, he built a pile of junk. He got angry and tossed the mess aside.

"I had a pretty good weekend," I said, "It wasn't quite what I expected, but I-"

"I don't want to hear it, Trevor," Carolina said. "I'm sorry, not now."

Marge groaned her disapproval.

The front door gasped open.

"Carolina, can you come outside for a second?"

Carolina's foot dug into my leg as she got up and turned the corner.

Goose bumps spilled over my arm and I squirmed as a shiver ran up my spine.

Chapter 19

The disc slid into the CD drive as I braked for the red light. The rolling rhythms of an electric guitar burst from the speaker and, within seconds, Bob Dylan's unmistakable croon flooded the car. Dark clouds covered the sky. To my right, the lake's waves splashed hard onto the shoreline.

Carolina's fingers flew over her phone's cracked screen. Her glasses reflected the glow.

I glanced at her phone. A text message filled the screen but I could not see from whom before the light turned green. I pressed on the pedal and the car picked up speed.

"Have you heard this album before?" I asked.

"Hold on a second. I'm nearly done."

Side Two

Carolina clicked another sentence, locked the screen, and tossed the phone into her glittering blue Betsey purse.

The guitars banged a conclusion and slinked into the second song.

"Okay, sorry, what'd you ask?

Carolina grabbed my free hand off my thigh. We held each other's palms.

"Have you heard this before? It's Dylan's *Bringing It All Back Home*."

"No, I haven't," Carolina said, "But fuck, I know this song. You sang that opening line over and over yesterday."

I turned the volume up two notches.

"She's got everything she needs, she's an artist, she don't look back," I spurted in my best impression of Dylan's wheeze. "She's got EVERYTHING she needs," I repeated, only louder and wheezier, "She's an artist, she don't look back."

Carolina turned down the music.

"I swear, Trevor, you don't want to know what will happen if I hear that line again."

The song finished.

I'm Not There

In the silence between tracks, I whispered, "She's got everything she neeeeeds-"

"Trevor, don't, I swear to god."

Carolina twisted my middle and index finger.

"Okay, okay," I yelped.

I pulled my hand away and grabbed hold of the wheel.

Dylan's band plugged into full force and let loose a strong, forceful beat behind the poet.

"Are you hungry, or anything?" I asked.

Carolina shook her head, crossed her arms, and rested her head against the the car door.

I nodded along with the beat.

After a two-minute silence, I said, "This was the first album he recorded with an electric band. He got tired of the folk scene and decided to follow his heart. So only three years after being heralded a major folk prophet, he ditched the topical songs and took up this rock and roll absurdism. At the time, it totally baffled the world."

Carolina nodded. I turned up the radio a notch and slowed the car down to 40 kilometers as we passed a school zone.

Side Two

"Can you imagine if some big time star dropped her dance crap all of a sudden and made something genuinely lo-fi? It would be like that."

"This doesn't sound that outrageous," Carolina said.

"Remember that back in the 60s, rock and roll was only teenager music. Not the genre for any man of greatness like Bobby Zimmerman."

"Would you want to be the great Dylan?"

"I'd give anything to have my signature on even ten of his songs. But I don't think that I'd want to be him."

"Why not?"

"Hell, I still don't even know who I am, or who I want to be. I don't want to say it's Dylan I'd want to be."

"Yeah, I know," Carolina said, "But like, do you-"

"Would I like to have lived that life? I don't know. He lived a weird life. I would've done things differently but it's impossible to answer. I'm looking at it from a different perspective than living it, you know?"

"True, Trevor. Yeah."

Carolina stared out the window as we passed into downtown Paterson. Only a few cars parked along the main road. I came to a stop sign. A mother pushed a carriage and held a little girl's hand while they crossed the street. The little girl wore a bright pink jacket zipped up to her chin. She walked right beside her mother. After they crossed, I took off.

I let the fourth song play through. When it ended, I asked, "What's the matter?"

"Nothing."

I turned the volume down. Carolina pulled her phone from her purse, unlocked it, and clicked away atop the glass screen.

A raindrop fell on the windshield. I turned left onto Asirriquan Road, which brought us through a neighbourhood of small, white houses adorned with great yards and thuggish trees.

Carolina sighed.

"Can we listen to something else?"

"Can we just hear the last few songs, and then we can listen to anything you want? Is that cool?"

Side Two

Another raindrop splashed onto the windshield. I looked up to the blackened sky. The only light came from the street lamps every few feet.

"Do you want to stop somewhere?"

"Where? It's going to pour any minute."

"We might get lucky."

"We're out of luck, Trevor."

After a pause, Carolina said, "Why don't you go home and write? We've got nothing to do and you don't want to waste your summer, right?"

I screwed up my face and said, "No. I want to chill with you. Why don't we see a movie or something?"

Carolina shrugged. "Whatever you want."

The car passed over a speed bump as we drove by Bong's convenience store. Carolina slipped her phone into her purse. I skipped to the last song and raised the volume.

"This song is probably Dylan's masterpiece. I'd give up anything to write about love and life this genuinely."

Carolina cranked the stereo until Dylan's ragged yelling and his rock and roll blasted from

I'm Not There

the speakers and invaded the space between us.

Chapter 20

I sat down and placed my rum and Coke beside my laptop. Ice cubes bobbed at the brink of the dark sea. The drink prepared me for a milestone.

Earlier in the day, I compiled and typed all my writing from the summer. All combined, the book stood at 145 pages. Most of the stories were first drafts, and I included a few I knew I would cut, but I felt accomplished.

I lifted the drink to my lips. My tongue danced as the harsh liquid passed through my throat. I pulled the glass from my lips.

150 pages. By the end of the day, I'd have 150 pages. With one month of summer left, I saw my 200-page book as a real possibility.

Side Two

I drank more rum and Coke, set the cup down, and opened a blank page on my computer. I centered the font, set to underline, and typed, "The New Story." I skipped six lines, justified my text to the left, and indented.

My phone vibrated on the arm of the brown chair. I got up and approached the chair.

Carolina calling.

I grabbed the phone and set it to silence. I told Carolina I needed to focus on writing and that I wouldn't answer the phone.

The phone vibrated again. I pressed silence again, placed it on the chair, and walked back to my desk.

I typed onto the blank page: "The raccoon fell onto its nose and barked."

The words meant nothing but they broke the spell of the blank page.

I skipped to the next line.

The phone rang again. I walked over. Carolina again. I picked the phone up and my finger hovered over the answer button. I frowned, set the phone down, and sat down at my desk.

I'm Not There

I deleted the raccoon line and opened the folder at the bottom of the screen marked "Summer Work." I clicked the file named "Ideas."

A five-page list of unused story ideas opened. As I read the notes, the stories flashed in my mind all over again. Finally, at the bottom of the second page, a one-line idea caught me.

"On a date with Carolina, she confesses about having cheated on me with the Rolling Stones."

I re-opened the blank page. I erased the existing title and wrote, "Trattorio's." That was the name of the restaurant Carolina and Trevor went to for their date. I used Carolina and I in most of my stories, but I knew she would recognize the fiction.

The story began as Trevor ordered chicken wings. Carolina ordered Goats Head Soup.

Somehow, a page filled. Four pages left. Carolina brought up the Stones concert.

My cell phone vibrated. My chair squeaked as I spun it. With each vibration, the phone inched closer to the edge until it plopped onto the seat of the chair with the screen flipped down.

Side Two

I turned back to my story and wrote another line.

I'm not an asshole. I can't pick up.

I deleted the line.

But what if it's important?

I stared at the page until the computer glare stung my eyes. I looked away and blinked rapidly.

I needed music.

I dropped to the floor to scan my record collection but I got up and plopped myself onto the desk chair without picking one.

Come on, Trevor. No distractions. Write the damn pages.

I picked up the story again.

"Trev, I need to tell you something," Carolina said.

Trevor thought Carolina had gone to the movies with a girlfriend the night the Stones concert rolled into town.

After Carolina tumbled the dice and revealed the truth, Trevor dropped a saucy chicken wing onto his lap.

I gave Carolina a monologue. She alternated

between bursts of tears for her betrayal and remembrances of great, albeit wrinkled, things past.

Within an hour, the story reached five pages. Carolina agreed to introduce Trevor to the Stones. The relationship stood on rocky grounds, but if he could get *Exile* signed by Charlie, all would be all right.

I typed "The End". My heart beat hard against my chest. I stared at the simple words and drained my drink.

150 pages. I needed a new glass.

I walked to the kitchen and made another rum and Coke. I used a taller cup and added two shots.

I returned to my office and sat at my desk.

The ceiling fan blurred as it brought cool waves of air onto me.

I sipped my drink and winced. I dropped the glass onto the desk, crossed the room, and knelt to pick out a CD. The choice came easy: Broken Social Scene's *You Forget It In People*. I walked back to the desk and threw the CD case onto the

Side Two

wooden top. It clattered loudly.

My cell phone vibrated. I spun to look at it. As I spun, my hand knocked against my glass. A heavy glob of rum and Coke streamed over the rim onto my keyboard.

My heart pounded. I searched the room for something to wipe the keyboard with. As I gave up, my eyes caught a folded blue facecloth at the back corner of the desk. I reached over and grabbed it. As I pulled my hand back, my arm knocked the glass over.

The entire drink poured onto my keyboard. The screen shot to a black gloss. The computer fan stopped humming. My eyes widened.

I ran the face cloth over the keyboard. The blue threads quickly turned to black.

I whispered, "Shit, shit, shit," under my breath. I tossed the soaked cloth aside, reached down, and pulled off my charcoal sock. I wiped the sock across the keyboard. The sock soaked up most of the Coke.

I reluctantly pressed the power button.

Nothing happened.

I pressed the button again.

The whisperings of "Shit" became mutters. These mutters evolved into shouts.

I stood up and paced the room. The carpet caught my hammerous footsteps.

Just like that, the stories no longer existed. Sure, some were hand-written, but those were first drafts.

I walked over to the big brown couch, picked up my phone, and slumped into the cushion.

I shut my eyes. The cushioning did not help. The weight of the summer pressed onto my shoulders.

The phone vibrated. Carolina.

I picked it up. "Hey."

"My god, you actually picked up."

I sighed. "You won't fucking believe it. I was writing the story that added up to my 150th page. After I finished, I traveled downstairs to fix a drink. When I returned, I spilt the fucking drink onto my keyboard. The computer died. Seriously, the computer went completely blank. I lost most of the stories. Even worse, if the com-

Side Two

puter is dead, I lost what I need to write the stories. I sure as hell am not writing a 200-page book with my bare hands. Goddammit."

Carolina stayed silent but I heard her breathe.

"I'm pretty pissed, to say the least," I said after a while, "But whatever. What's with all the calls? I told you I couldn't talk."

After a few more seconds, Carolina said, "My sister got in a car accident. I needed you to watch Marco while my parents and I went to check on her."

Carolina's voice cracked as she said, "I stayed to watch him instead."

I stared at the black screen.

"I'm... So sorry, Carolina. Really. My god, I'm sorry. I had no idea obviously. If I had have known... But wait, how is she?"

"She's okay," Carolina said.

"Good, good."

I looked down. I tapped the power button.

"I've got to go," Carolina said.

"Wait, no, hold on-"

Carolina said, "No," and hung up.

Chapter 21

Carolina and I waited on a bench at the end of Platform 3 at the Paterson train station. Early afternoon, the clear sky harboured a breezeless, humid day. The stale smell of cigarettes and McDonalds carried over from four benches down. A man and a woman traded a burning cigarette for half a chicken nugget. No more than ten people stood over the whole stretch of the platform.

I wiped sweat off my forehead, dried it on my jeans, and grabbed Carolina's leg.

Carolina pulled her pink ear bud out and said, "Yeah?"

"Oh, it was nothing."

Carolina tucked her ear bud back in. Mine fell

Side Two

out. The screechy rumbling of construction in the parking lot on the other side of the tracks escalated. I snatched the dangling ear bud and stuck it into my ear. The beats of Carolina's rap muffled out most of the construction buzz.

Down the track, head lights blasted. A group of three teenagers raced to the yellow line along the edge of the platform.

I pulled my ear bud out and nudged Carolina. She didn't turn her head. I nudged her again and pointed to the train.

Carolina stood up, picked up her purse from the seat beside her, and draped it over her shoulder.

"Will we have time for dinner before the show?" Carolina asked.

"Yeah, sure," I said. "Are you in the mood for anything in particular?"

"Not really."

I chuckled.

"We'll figure that out once we're in Toronto. I've got to tell you Carolina, I'm looking forward to a night out in the city. When was the last time we went? June? May even?"

I leaned in closer to Carolina.

"It'll be good to relax. I stressed out about that damn book way too much. This concert is what I need."

"Well good," Carolina said, "Congratulations."

I turned my head to face Carolina's pale cheek. Her eye stayed stationed straight ahead.

"Are you alright?"

Carolina nodded. "I'm fine."

I sighed and shook my head.

"Did you want to listen to the Folk? It might be good to know what to expect."

The green and white train screeched as it halted. We walked to the yellow line. The train stopped with a door directly in front of us.

The doors hissed open. I followed Carolina through the thin corridor to the top floor. We sat in the seats immediately at the top of the stairs. Carolina sat by the window. I sat by the aisle.

"Did you want to hear the Folk?" I repeated.

"No, it's fine."

The train doors shut and the announcer said

Side Two

that the next station would be Lowell. The next station stop is Lowell station.

Chapter 22

I cut through the gravel path behind St. Raymond's, my elementary school. The empty playground seemed significantly smaller than I remembered.

Rain drizzled atop my head. I didn't bother wiping my streaked glasses. I just wanted to meet Thom for a few beers at Izzy's Pub and forget the week. I wanted to order an overpriced pint from a new waitress because Izzy's always featured a new waitress. Some things never stayed the same.

At the end of the path, I turned onto the sidewalk of Descendant's Crescent.

My pocket vibrated. I pulled my cell phone

Side Two

out and answered, "Hello?"

"Trevor," Carolina whispered, "Could you come over for a bit?"

"Right now? I can't. I'm on my way to meet Thom."

"Oh."

"Why? What's up?"

"It's nothing. We've just got to talk later, okay?"

I stopped, straightened my back, and tightened my grip around the phone.

"No Carolina, tell me what's up?"

Carolina stayed silent for a moment until she whispered, "I've just done a lot of thinking the last few days."

I didn't say anything.

"Oh Trevor, I know you've felt it too. Nothing is the way it used to be. Things are off. I just- I just think we'd be best off if we ended things now, before things got actually bad."

I sat on the edge of someone's hard lawn.

"You actually want to end this?"

"No, but I think we need to," Carolina whispered. "It isn't working anymore."

"I...I don't know what to say."

"Tell me what you're thinking Trevor. Please, tell me what you're thinking."

I held my head up by my right hand. The skin above my eye pulled back. The sidewalk slowly succumbed to the splatters of the rain.

"Trevor?"

"I don't know. I know what you mean but I'm just fucking surprised, you know?"

"I know Trevor. I just think that this is for the best. For both of us. We can talk later, but I need to go. What are you going to do now?"

"I guess I should still meet Thom for a drink."

Carolina sighed.

"Goodbye Trevor."

I slid the phone into my pocket. I got up and tramped to Izzy's. The rain picked up along the way.

When I walked in, Thom sat at a booth near the back, beside the entrance to the patio. We were the only customers. I plunked myself across from him.

Side Two

Thom put the menu down and said, "Hey man."

"Hey."

"What's going on?"

I sighed and looked at the dark spots on my pants.

"Carolina and I broke up."

The waitress came over from the bar. A redhead for the first time.

"Can I get you something?"

I looked up, paused, shook my head and said, "Just a pint. Whatever's domestic."

The waitress walked to the bar.

"What the fuck," Thom said. "When?"

"She just called me ten minutes ago."

"Shit."

Thom sipped his beer.

"Yeah."

"How are you uhh, doing?"

The waitress set my beer on a coaster and walked back behind the bar. The foamy head of the beer took up nearly half the glass.

Chapter 23

Thom offered to drive me home after the beer if I waited while he downed a glass of water. I declined. The rain lightened to nearly nothing. When I got home, I walked immediately upstairs to my office.

I flicked on the ceiling fan. Only one bulb lit. Shadows crawled over the room except for the TV in the corner. I closed the blinds before I sat down and spun my computer chair to face the desk.

I opened my laptop. A thick layer of dust covered the terminally black screen, like I'd never cleaned it. I swiped a tissue across but the dust only streaked unevenly. I crumpled the tis-

Side Two

sue and tossed it onto the keyboard. I shut the screen and sat down on the carpet, in front of the records.

I lay on my back. I let my eyes close. I let time pass. I let my mind fall blank and I let the night skip forward and I wanted to let the night disappear and let tomorrow begin but I knew the night wouldn't let me escape so I sat up. I put my finger to the beginning of the record collection and began the familiar flipthrough.

My hope for salvation nearly reached an end when Springsteen's haunted gaze caught my heavy eyes. He leaned back on floral wallpaper and his pain shot right into me.

The record slipped into my hand and I set it carefully on the turntable. I lifted the needle, placed it on the edge, and flicked on the speakers. Weinberg's drums kicked in.

Darkness on the Edge of Town began.

I hoisted myself up, walked over to the big soft brown chair, and plunged into it.

My pocket notebook lay open on the stool beside the chair. I grabbed the notebook and tossed it onto the desk. I couldn't write anything tonight when only poison could pour from my pen. Enough poison already existed in the world.

As the pop strains and jangling pianos of the fourth song's chorus roared, I sat on the ground with my back against the chair. My left leg extended over the line that divided the room from light and shadow. My foot bathed in the warm golden light. The rest of my body huddled in the depth of darkness. My hands resting on my erect knee, the song ended.

A hard yet soothing piano line rang out. A pause, and the piano line repeated. My eyes, ears, and mind perked up. I nearly smiled.

Bruce's hollow, bare voice emerged. The piano line repeated as Bruce sang his tale of racing in his car, running with his lady, blowing out with his first heat in the summer when the time was right. Him and his girl escaped onto the highway, where the sights were everything. Max came in with a simple drumbeat. The song burst alive.

I bobbed my head, shut my eyes, and inhaled deeply. I wrapped my arms around my

Side Two

legs as Bruce went racing in the streets. The piano pounded, an organ chimed, and drums beat swiftly. Bruce howled over it all.

The music overwhelmed me and I needed everything — the instruments, the song, the record player, the room, the night, this summer, and this sad poor suburban life — to give up and blow away. Just then, every instrument disappeared except the piano. I sighed and tried to smile but I couldn't.

Halfway through the next verse, a harmony of broken hearts sang behind Bruce. As Bruce went racing in the streets with his summer girl for the final time, the music carried on. The piano played out its final cries while the drums stuck to their steady beat. The needle lifted and just like that, the song ended.

I crawled to the record player, placed the needle back at the beginning of "Racing in the Streets", and lay on the carpet.

The piano rang out, as it always would.

"At least there's that," I thought.

Chapter 24

Whether it was Sister Ray or the rain or the ill-informed self-confidence that beer brought on, I don't know, but it struck me that the night, Thom's last Saturday in Paterson before he moved back to Toronto for Second year, needed to be graced by real live rock and roll.

"Let's record an album," I mumbled.

I leaned over to the case of beer on the kitchen floor and snatched a bottle. I cracked it open, tossed the lid across Thom's table, and drank two gulps.

Louder, I said, "Let's go downstairs. We need to record something."

"You got some ideas, do ya?" Thom replied.

Side Two

I got up, walked into the adjoining living room, and picked up the acoustic guitar that leaned against the leather couch. I weaved back to the kitchen and sat the guitar on my thigh.

Thom watched me carefully. His uncle passed the guitar onto Thom at a young age. I grabbed a pick off the table and strummed a D chord.

Finally, I said, "There's no one idea, per se. Y'know, I think that we could just jam. Let's make it up as we go along."

I moved my hands along the neck. I altered my fingers into different positions, but each time I strummed, something sounded off. I passed the guitar to Thom. He played the opening chords of "Rocky Raccoon".

"Do you want to call anyone else to play?"

"Fuck it," I said, "Let's just do this on our own."

I picked up the case of beer and grabbed my notebook. Thom choked his guitar and followed me as I traveled down the circular staircase into Thom's basement.

A snake's nest of wires spread across the concrete basement floor. Hand-written chord arrangements on yellow sheets surrounded both amplifiers, which were a few feet apart from each other. A white binder spewed more papers onto the green couch. Thom's devil- red electric guitar sat on a stand beside the largest amplifier. Another electric blue guitar lay on the floor, in front of the couch.

"How're we going to do this, brother?"

"Just ask yourself," I said, as I set the two four down, "What would Uncle Lou do?"

I passed Thom a beer. He set it aside.

"Alright, alright, alright," I said, "I got it. Thom, you'll play the acoustic. We'll keep some sort of rhythm going, some melody. And I'll just fucking destroy it with noise. Deal?"

Thom laughed and responded, "Lou wouldn't have it any other way."

I laughed too. "Unless we just unleash an onslaught of noise and make a fucking *Metal Machine Music* for the twenty first century."

"You think we've got that power, brother?"

I got up, ignoring his comment, but not be-

Side Two

fore I popped open another beer. I flicked on Thom's amplifier. An extraordinary wave of distortion discharged.

As Thom fiddled with his red four-track recorder, I picked up Thom's sapphire guitar and pulled the strap around my neck. The guitar hung loosely. I replaced the cable in Thom's amp with my own.

I strummed the guitar. A few clear patches of noise poured out. I punched the button on the amp to unleash the heavy distortion. I strummed a few more times.

"Are there any songs you want to do?" I asked.

"Do you know any?"

I laughed.

"You ready?"

"Let's go, brother."

Thom pressed record. I struck a single note on the guitar. I nearly tripped as I rushed up to the amp. The distortion grew louder and louder with each clumsy step. The initial wave of noise stabilized into a heady, high-pitched drone.

Under the siren, Thom played the acoustic

I'm Not There

guitar. His head hung low so his curly shag hid his face.

Thom struck some of the most unusual chords that I'd heard him play in a long time. I responded by sending off another wave of distortion. I held down my strings and sipped my warm beer. I set the bottle beside the couch. Thom continued his melody and we jammed that groove for four minutes. My noise provided a backdrop for Thom's aggressively skilled playing.

Thom shifted into a separate, faster melody. I took this chance to strike more notes and slide my fingers along the strings. I waved the guitar back and forth from the amplifier, dragging noise in and out. I followed a beat in my head and slammed my pick hard on the steel strings. Thom combated me by striking his acoustic harder. His skill and melody overpowered my sheer, senseless noise. I nearly lost my head a few times and quit, but the beat didn't let me loose. I hit a single high note and stunted my strings.

Thom carried on. The acoustic crashed on the soundscape. For a second, I considered dropping

Side Two

the electric altogether and letting Thom take over.

I sauntered to the couch, leaned down, and searched through the binder of papers. Most pages had chords but I grabbed the first one with words. Thom looked up, saw the paper, and struck a slow, stirring melody with picked notes in between strums.

I whispered a countdown from five. At one, I sang, my voice deep but unsure. My voice didn't align with the music whatsoever. The words worked even worse. I searched the page for the chorus. When I identified the song, I flung the sheet aside and hung my head.

Luckily, Thom carried on, fully committed. He sang a crawling cover of Neil Young's "Heart of Gold".

As Thom declared that he'd been to Hollywood, I crashed in on my guitar. The amplifier emitted a blast of noise. Thom struck down hard and changed his melody. For the first time, I allowed myself to let loose. I closed my eyes and felt myself getting in tune with Thom. For what felt like hours but turned out to be just over ten minutes, Thom and I entered a total state of noise confusion. I ripped apart the guitar and let everything out.

Near the end, I felt the beat disappear. I ripped a few more chords before I pulled the strap over my head and leaned the guitar in front of the amp. Feedback wavered in and out with shocking force. I smiled tiredly at the perfection that leaked from the amp. Thom strummed a closing melody line, repeated it, and placed his guitar down. In this noise-drenched conclusion, Thom hit stop on the recording.

My arms were sore and heavy. I leaned back onto the couch and pulled a beer to my lips. It felt colder. Thom turned off the amp. Silence shot through the room.

Thom looked at me for the first time since recording begun.

"How was that for you, brother?"

"That did it, man. How long were we going for?"

Thom leaned over to the recorder. "21 min-

Side Two

utes."

"My god. What are we going to do with it?"

"Are we done?"

"That's it, brother, that's all there was to it. What'd you think?"

"That was something," Thom said. "Definitely different than anything else I've recorded."

"Let's send it to all the major labels and music magazines. Maybe we got it, eh?"

Thom looked quizzically at the recording. "Shit, if that makes it before any of my band's recordings... But hey, at least one of us finished an album this summer."

I pulled my phone from my pocket, checked the time, and shoved it back in.

"I thought you were nearly done?"

Thom shook his head. "I've got about ten songs recorded, but I don't know. It's just not ready."

Thom shrugged. "I'll keep trucking on it during the school year. At least with my apartment, I'll have a space to practice during the semester. Lord knows I've got time until classes start."

I'm Not There

Thom turned off the four-track.

"I can't believe I go back to Toronto on Tuesday. For four months, the summer flew by."

I picked up my guitar and strummed a few times.

"What's going on in your mind?" Thom asked.

I looked up, caught Thom's eye, and sighed.

"I- I just don't know where this music came from. It wasn't there half an hour ago, and now it is. I'm just wired from that surge."

Thom shook his head. "Music comes from either your head or your soul. That definitely was not head music, so it must have been your soul. Heart break will force it out of any man."

I sipped my beer and wondered what Carolina would think of the album.

Chapter 25

My head leaned against the chipped white doorframe. Goose bumps crawled up my crossed arms under my ratty white T-shirt.

Carolina stood at the edge of my front steps, under a wall of rain. Her dyed-black hair lay curled over the shoulders of her velvet jacket. She stared up at me.

"Did you call me over just to look at me or to invite me in?"

I picked up a soggy Paterson Polar paper off the freshly painted porch and stepped backwards into the house. Carolina walked up the creaky stairs and stepped inside. I shut the door behind her.

Side Two

Carolina slipped off unfamiliar tan gloves and placed them on the wooden shelf. She hung her jacket on the railing by the door.

"I can't stay long."

"I know. Did you want to come in for a, uh, drink?"

I motioned towards the kitchen.

Carolina sniffled. "Is that all you called me over for, Trevor?"

"No, no, not at all."

She didn't say anything.

"One drink, Carolina?"

"Okay."

Carolina slid off her blackened Uggs and walked into the kitchen. I pulled a thin CD case from my pocket, slipped it into her jacket pocket, and hurried to the kitchen.

Carolina sat at the circular glass kitchen table. I fixed us each a screwdriver, tossed in a few chunks of ice, stirred, and set the glasses down on the table. Carolina didn't touch hers but I sat down and gulped back a mouthful.

"How have you been?" I asked, after I swallowed.

Carolina's eyes tightened and she squeezed her cup.

"What was up with that blog post you posted? About laying down and being born again? Did you find God or something since school started?"

"Oh, no," I said. "That's from a song."

I took another sip.

"Just a song?"

"Just a song."

My head toppled and my eyes shut.

Carolina sighed. My foot tapped on the tile. I looked up at Carolina. She had finally taken a sip of her drink.

"Carolina, I know what you're going to say, but can we try and talk? I want to tell you everything that you need to hear and that I need to say."

"Fine Trevor, talk. I came over to hear what you'd have to say."

I sipped my drink. I didn't know where to start. I skipped between all the options in my

Side Two

head.

"Do you know what you're going to say, Trevor?" Carolina asked. "I gave you every day of our relationship to tell me what you needed. Or about how you felt. You never could, or you never did. I don't know."

I lowered my head.

Carolina sighed. She placed a hand on my cheek and guided me to look up at her. I glimpsed into her red eyes and turned my body away again. Carolina let go of my cheek to dry her own face.

"Trevor, just promise me that you're going to do what's important. For once. Do what you need to do. Meditate. Figure out what's wrong. When you're ready to talk, you know I'm here."

Carolina's cell phone rang. The melody sounded like Dylan, but it couldn't be. She turned towards the front door, pulled the phone from her front pocket, and shut it off.

"I have to go but Trevor, if we're supposed to be together, we will be. Don't lose sight of that. We can't plan everything. Let's just see."

Carolina swallowed a big gulp of her drink

I'm Not There

and stood up.

Carolina walked to the entrance. I followed her and leaned against the beige wall. She slid on her boots and her jacket, hesitated, and hugged me.

Carolina let go and said, "Goodbye."

I smiled but I pleaded she could read my eyes.

Carolina nodded, inhaled, and walked out the door. The patter of each step down the driveway shook my body. I looked at the shelf.

"You forgot your gloves!" I shouted.

Carolina kept walking. I scrunched the gloves into a tight ball. I stood at the doorway until Carolina slid into the passenger's seat of the orange sports car parked across the street. I put the gloves back onto the shelf and shut the door.

I placed the record on the turntable, hovered the needle over the edge, and dropped the lever. The needle lowered onto the last groove and locked in.

I brought a thick, white joint to my lips and lit it. A puff of smoke lifted off as the guitar swam

Side Two

into the sound stream. I rose, stepped back, and took another hit. The thin rolling paper faded away. I weaved through the room and shut the curtains.

Van Morrison sang about a romance damned from the start. I lay on the big brown chair and caught every word. Sucking on the joint, stretching my legs, I closed my eyes and nearly heard her, felt her, smelt her beside me.

Van declared that she would take me into her arms again. I loathed him for lying. The only arms for me now would be in the arms of a dream.

I whispered to her, "You can search way up into the Heavens and down to the islands of Hell, and through every crack along the way, but there's not a stranger in this world that loves you more than I love you."

As the words slipped from my mouth, they joined the smoke and took on life as ghosts — free and lost forever.

I rose from the chair, grabbed the gloves, and ran through the front door. It slammed behind me and I found myself on a silent street with a

I'm Not There

full bloom tree on the lawn of each gated house, in another tired old town, in another world. A sign on the iron fence in front of my house read "Cyprus Avenue."

Van lay on the grass along the street and rested his back on the thick trunk of a pine tree. He whispered to himself and looked up at the mansion on the hill.

I pulled myself up off the ground. I ran my hands over the coarse bark of the tree. I looked past the mansion. A cardinal streaked by and punctured the cool gray slate of the world — a world consumed by blue pain that left no one unscathed or unmarked — and I followed the cardinal until it disappeared into the clouds.

My eyes fell onto the porch of the mansion. Carolina knocked on the mile-high doors.

I yelled, "I'm not there!" and tried to race to the mansion but my feet locked onto the asphalt and would not budge. Carolina stepped off the porch and walked around to the back of the house. She disappeared behind a gate of trees.

I turned around to go home but my house

Side Two

no longer existed. Carolina's gloves fell from my hand and landed in the cushion of grass.

I reached for the gloves but the needle lifted off the record.

I stared at the ceiling. My heart pounded as I rose from the chair and squished the roach into an ashtray.

I flipped the record to the second side and dropped the needle. I sat at my desk and started my laptop. Carolina sat beside me and ran her fingers through the waves in my dark hair.

I imagined another time, another place.

I typed, "Every time I see you, I just don't know what to do." The words burst from the screen and I couldn't help but continue to write.

I pulled open the curtains and looked out the window. Carolina walked up the driveway. Her hands dug deep in her pockets.

Carolina smiled and I smiled back at her.

I closed the computer, opened the front door, and welcomed her in.

About the Author

Matt Long is a graduate of the
Professional Writing program at the
University of Toronto Mississauga.
Born in Quebec, he moved to Ontario
at the age of 7.
The Velvet Underground are
his favourite band.
This is Matt Long's first novella.

I'm Not There
is the first in a series of stories
chronicling the lives of
the Coltrain family
and their hometown of
Paterson, Ontario.

Made in the USA
Charleston, SC
01 June 2013